READY OR NOT
HERE COME FOURTEEN FRIGHTENING STORIES!

READY OR NOT

HERE COME FOURTEEN FRIGHTENING STORIES!

Chosen by JOAN KAHN

Greenwillow Books, New York

Library of Congress Cataloging-in-Publication Data

Ready or not.
Summary: A collection of fourteen unsettling
tales by a variety of authors.
1. Horror tales, American. 2. Horror tales, English.
[1. Horror stories.   2. Short stories]   I. Kahn, Joan.
PZ5.R1989   1987   [Fic]   86-31875
ISBN 0-688-07167-8

CONTENTS

ACKNOWLEDGMENTS

We gratefully acknowledge the following permissions:

COLLIER ASSOCIATES: "The Girl in the Mirror" by Margot Arnold. Copyright © 1976 by Margot Arnold. Reprinted by permission of Collier Associates, Literary Agents.

DON CONGDON ASSOCIATES, INC.: "The Playground" by Ray Bradbury originally appeared in *Esquire*. Copyright © 1953 by Esquire Inc. and renewed 1981 by Ray Bradbury. Reprinted by permission of Don Congdon Associates, Inc.

CURTIS BROWN GROUP LIMITED: "A Private Ghost" from *Spring Song and Other Stories* by Joyce Cary. Copyright © 1960 by Michael Joseph Ltd. Reprinted by permission of the Literary Estate of Joyce Cary.

CURTIS BROWN, LTD." "Robert" from *The Blessington Method* by Stanley Ellin. Copyright © 1958 by Stanley Ellin. Reprinted by permission of Curtis Brown, Ltd.

ARTHUR B. GREENE: "Peter Two" from *Tips on a Dead Jockey* by Irwin Shaw originally appeared in *The New Yorker*. Copyright © 1946, 1952, 1953, 1954, 1955, 1956, 1959 by Irwin Shaw. Reprinted by permission of The Estate of Irwin Shaw.

CENTURY HUTCHINSON LIMITED: "The Vinegar Mother" from *The Fallen Curtain* by Ruth Rendell. Copyright © 1976 by Ruth Rendell. Reprinted by permission of The Hutchinson Publishing Group, an imprint of Century Hutchinson Limited.

LITERISTIC, LTD.: "A Hell of a Story" by H. R. F. Keating. Copyright © 1972 by H. R. F. Keating. Reprinted by permission of Literistic, Ltd.

INTRODUCTION

Imagination. It's what every good author uses—what every good author expects his readers to have. Some of us have more of it, some of us have less, but nobody (nobody who enjoys reading) has none.

Real life has much in it that is truly frightening, but not *always* frightening, thank goodness, and so very often we like our reading to stir our imagination, to make us feel there's something *really* scary, scarier than real life, creeping up behind us. It's the author's job to make us believe, to make the hair on our heads stand straight up—for a while.

Here are some very good authors whose stories will raise the hair on your head. Read about Mr. Pucker and the tiny footsteps he kept hearing, about Rodney, who rode with Margaret even if the social worker said he mustn't, and about Mr. Wellman, who wasn't nice to cats.

There are lots of other good and frighteningly imaginative stories in this collection. If *your* imagination is any good at all, watch out! There just might be something coming up behind you.

READY OR NOT

HERE COME FOURTEEN FRIGHTENING STORIES!

HAYES WILSON

Please, No Strawberries

His mother told him not to turn on the TV set; it would soon be time for him to go to school. She herself left well before it was light, and his present father, the man who now lived in their house, had gone to work at some hour in the night. His other father, the real one, was dead. The blood had run out of him in little rivers and they had come to take him away, never to return.

Sometimes he felt that his father, the first one, was watching from somewhere in the dark, even though he knew that life must run out with all that blood. It was something that could happen to you if you were not on the watch all the time. Guns, knives, probably lots of things could make that red liquid inside you move out.

Cautiously he moved toward the TV; cautiously he turned the knob. His mother, that tall woman who moved easily and sometimes threateningly through his nights and part of his days, would have no way to know that he had turned on the set. She was at work, and he was scared,

1

scared of seeing his father again with the bright red blood running out. The new father meant nothing to him although the man laughed and talked with the big woman his mother.

It was she who took him on his first day to whatever school he was currently attending. He knew that many schools did not want him. He had heard them say that they could not cope. What was cope?

In class the teacher tried to persuade him to look at the board, to speak as the others spoke, to recite words, words, words. He wanted to run loose in the room, to yell, to keep on the move. Even in the bright classroom some shadow might emerge, might pursue him. Blood was inside everybody, every living creature, and if anything got to him—

He turned on the TV and watched intently as the light came on and then a man was talking about some foolishness, he did not know what. This picture meant nothing special to him although he could see the man hold something up, perhaps toothpaste, from the way he was showing his own teeth, very white in his pink face. The rest of the room was still dark; it was the quality he hated most about winter.

Would blood freeze, he wondered, if it ran out of you in winter? He went to the kitchen, walking warily along in the dark to examine the knife that lay near the top in a kitchen drawer.

Soon the school bus would come honking along. The driver always tooted this way in winter, and as he lived in the last house on the block he often waited until he heard the sound before he left the familiar dark for the alien outside. He was supposed to leave when the alarm went off. His mother had set it, but she could not know that he waited sometimes for the sound of the bus. Then he ran.

He turned the TV set off with a click before taking off for his place on the bus, hoping that no one started a fight this morning. Usually they rode through the gloomy streets to a far place without incident, arriving at the new school where he was perfectly sure they would soon tell his mother that they could not cope. No one ever explained cope to him.

He had had nothing to eat when he left; he did not want the bowl of cold cereal left out to feed his skinny frame. At noon he would have the hot lunch, even if he had spent the morning evading any attempts to get him to say what the teacher wanted, even if he had run around the room looking for shadows and blood, but keeping to himself what moved him.

At noon the teacher would escort all of them to the lunchroom where other women would serve their plates, dolloping out mashed potatoes, meat, and always some green stuff. The teacher had tried to tell them that green stuff was good for them, but he had imitated the others. When the green was brocco—whatever the name was—they all pushed it aside, even the kids whose parents had come with money to pay for them to eat. Kids did not like brocco—whatever—and he was a kid, even though he was one with whom the school could not cope.

About strawberries he was uncertain. Last year at his school of that time some kids had eaten strawberries; some had pushed them off and had eaten the cake underneath. He considered the red a bit like blood, especially where the juice ran. It was not strawberry time in winter though, and maybe this school would not have shortcake.

He had once upset his plate with a clattering noise. Some kids had laughed, others had stared. It was over quickly, and fortunately nothing had spilled into his lap. Everyone

3

ate rapidly and soon they were all getting their wraps and going outdoors.

He had a pencil to which he sometimes talked if no one were watching or listening. "You sharp like a knife," he told it lovingly, "and you mine."

To keep it sharp he went often to the sharpener, more often than the teacher considered necessary although she rarely mentioned it. Was she coping?

He had sat in various offices—doctors' offices, principals' offices, offices of people whose place in the scheme of his life he did not understand. He knew only that he wanted to escape, that out there somewhere some large fear was ready to swallow him and that he could only run or make loud noises to try to fend it off.

Some day, he was sure, the blood would run out of him just as it had run out of his father. Only by being continually alert could he hope to keep himself whole.

The teacher said, "Look at the board." The teacher said, "Listen."

Words, numbers, projects; they were not his world.

One time melted into another . . . He heard the man in the office say that there should be some special place for him. Or was it just that he could not cope? His mother wanted them to try again; they said no. They were not equipped at this school to handle cases like him; they did not know what was the matter.

He had his sharp pencil in a pocket. He took it out and ran it across his wrist until bright red blood appeared. Then he laughed, and the big woman his mother and the man behind the desk looked at him.

"Oh, son," she screamed, "you've hurt yourself," and the man behind the desk said, "We'll put something on it. It isn't deep."

They did not understand that sooner or later he would bleed as his father had bled, his real father, the one who had been taken away by strange men. The only thing he could control was his pencil, which was his little knife, his cutting instrument, his possession whatever school he was in.

He rose to accompany his mother, who had left her work early to come for him. Outside the sun was shining now as he skipped along, scarcely paying attention as he heard her say, "I'm sure you could learn if you'd only try. I'm sure. I am so helpless."

No, you aren't, he thought. You aren't helpless. You have the knife in the kitchen drawer. And I have my sharp pencil, whose point can bring blood like strawberries with a lot of juice.

That's why you went away for a while. Because of what you did with the knife. My grandmother took care of me but she couldn't chase away the shadows. I saw. I heard. That was some fight you had. You used that knife. I can use my pencil. I can bring blood. Like my father's blood. Blood running like juice out of strawberries.

He danced ahead of her, temporarily unafraid of lurking shadows anywhere, not thinking of the morning to come when she would be gone again and he would be alone in the wintry darkness, waiting for the bus to take him to another school perhaps, another school that could not cope, another school with words, and projects, and brocco-whatever, but please, no strawberries.

IRWIN SHAW

Peter
Two

It was Saturday night and people were killing each other
by the hour on the small screen. Policemen were shot in
the line of duty, gangsters were thrown off roofs, and an
elderly lady was slowly poisoned for her pearls, and her
murderer brought to justice by a cigarette company after a
long series of discussions in the office of a private detective.
Brave, unarmed actors leaped at villains holding forty-fives,
and ingénues were saved from death by the knife by the
quick thinking of various handsome and intrepid young
men.

Peter sat in the big chair in front of the screen, his feet up
over the arm, eating grapes. His mother wasn't home, so he
ate the seeds and all as he stared critically at the violence
before him. When his mother was around, the fear of ap-
pendicitis hung in the air and she watched carefully to see
that each seed was neatly extracted and placed in an ash-
tray. Too, if she were home, there would be irritated little
lectures on the quality of television entertainment for the

young, and quick-tempered fiddling with the dials to find
something that was vaguely defined as educational. Alone,
daringly awake at eleven o'clock, Peter ground the seeds between his teeth, enjoying the impolite noise and the solitude
and freedom of the empty house. During the television
commercials Peter closed his eyes and imagined himself
hurling bottles at large unshaven men with pistols and walking slowly up dark stairways toward the door behind which
everyone knew the Boss was waiting, the bulge of his shoulder holster unmistakable under the cloth of his pencil-
striped flannel jacket.

Peter was thirteen years old. In his class there were three
other boys with the same given name, and the history
teacher, who thought he was a funny man, called them Peter One, Peter Two (now eating grapes, seeds and all), Peter
Three, and Peter the Great. Peter the Great was, of course,
the smallest boy in the class. He weighed only sixty-two
pounds, and he wore glasses, and in games he was always
the last one to be chosen. The class always laughed when
the history teacher called out "Peter the Great," and Peter
Two laughed with them, but he didn't think it was so
awfully funny.

He had done something pretty good for Peter the Great
two weeks ago, and now they were what you might call
friends. All the Peters were what you might call friends, on
account of that comedian of a history teacher. They weren't
real friends, but they had something together, something
the other boys didn't have. They didn't like it, but they had
it, and it made them responsible for each other. So two
weeks ago, when Charley Blaisdell, who weighed a hundred
and twenty, took Peter the Great's cap at recess and started
horsing around with it, and Peter the Great looked as if he
was going to cry, he, Peter Two, grabbed the cap and gave it

back and faced Blaisdell. Of course, there was a fight, and Peter thought it was going to be his third defeat of the term, but a wonderful thing happened. In the middle of the fight, just when Peter was hoping one of the teachers would show up (they sure showed up plenty of times when you didn't need them), Blaisdell let a hard one go. Peter ducked and Blaisdell hit him on the top of the head and broke his arm. You could tell right off he broke his arm, because he fell to the ground yelling, and his arm just hung like a piece of string. Walters, the gym teacher, finally showed up and carried Blaisdell off, yelling all the time, and Peter the Great came up and said admiringly, "Boy, one thing you have to admit, you sure have a hard head."

Blaisdell was out of class two days, and he still had his arm in the sling, and every time he was excused from writing on the blackboard because he had a broken arm, Peter got a nice warm feeling all over. Peter the Great hung around him all the time, doing things for him and buying him sodas, because Peter the Great's parents were divorced and gave him all the money he wanted, to make up to him. And that was okay.

But the best thing was the feeling he'd had since the fight. It was like what the people on the television must feel after they'd gone into a room full of enemies and come out with the girl or with the papers or with the suspect, leaving corpses and desolation behind them. Blaisdell weighed a hundred and twenty pounds but that hadn't stopped Peter any more than the fact that the spies all had two guns apiece ever stopped the F.B.I. men on the screen. They saw what they had to do and they went in and did it, that was all. Peter couldn't phrase it for himself, but for the first time in his life he had a conscious feeling of confidence and pride in himself.

"Let them come," he muttered obscurely, munching grape seeds and watching the television set through narrowed eyes, "just let them come."

He was going to be a dangerous man, he felt, when he grew up, but one to whom the weak and the unjustly hunted could safely turn. He was sure he was going to be six feet tall, because his father was six feet tall, and all his uncles, and that would help. But he would have to develop his arms. They were just too thin. After all, you couldn't depend on people breaking their bones on your head every time. He had been doing push-ups each morning and night for the past month. He could only do five and a half at a time so far, but he was going to keep at it until he had arms like steel bars. Arms like that really could mean the difference between life and death later on, when you had to dive under the gun and disarm somebody. You had to have quick reflexes, too, of course, and be able to feint to one side with your eyes before the crucial moment. And, most important of all, no matter what the odds, you had to be fearless. One moment of hesitation and it was a case for the morgue. But now, after the battle of Peter the Great's cap, he didn't worry about that part of it, the fearless part. From now on, it would just be a question of technique.

Comedians began to appear all over the dial, laughing with a lot of teeth, and Peter went into the kitchen and got another bunch of grapes and two tangerines from the refrigerator. He didn't put on the light in the kitchen and it was funny how mysterious a kitchen could be near midnight when nobody else was home, and there was only the beam of the light from the open refrigerator, casting shadows from the milk bottles onto the linoleum. Until recently he hadn't liked the dark too much and he always turned on lights wherever he went, but you had to practice being fearless, just like anything else.

He ate the two tangerines standing in the dark in the kitchen, just for practice. He ate the seeds, too, to show his mother. Then he went back into the living room, carrying the grapes.

The comedians were still on and still laughing. He fiddled with the dial, but they were wearing funny hats and laughing and telling jokes about the income tax on all the channels. If his mother hadn't made him promise to go to sleep by ten o'clock, he'd have turned off the set and gone to bed. He decided not to waste his time and got down on the floor and began to do push-ups, trying to be sure to keep his knees straight. He was up to four and slowing down when he heard the scream. He stopped in the middle of a push-up and waited, just to make sure. The scream came again. It was a woman and it was real loud. He looked up at the television set. There was a man there talking about floor wax, a man with a mustache and a lot of teeth, and it was a cinch *he* wasn't doing any screaming.

The next time the scream came there was moaning and talking at the end of it, and the sound of fists beating on the front door. Peter got up and turned off the television, just to be sure the sounds he was hearing weren't somehow being broadcast.

The beating on the door began again and a woman's voice cried "Please, please, *please* . . ." and there was no doubt about it anymore.

Peter looked around him at the empty room. Three lamps were lit and the room was nice and bright and the light was reflected off the grapes and off the glass of the picture of the boats on Cape Cod that his Aunt Martha painted the year she was up there. The television set stood in the corner, like a big blind eye now that the light was out. The cushions of the soft chair he had been sitting in to watch the programs were pushed in and he knew his mother would come and plump them out before she went to sleep, and the whole room looked like a place in which it was impossible to hear a woman screaming at midnight and beating on the door with her fists and yelling, "Please, please, *please* . . ."

The woman at the door yelled "Murder, murder, he's killing me!" and for the first time Peter was sorry his parents had gone out that night.

"Open the door!" the woman yelled. "Please, *please* open the door!" You could tell she wasn't saying please just to be polite by now.

Peter looked nervously around him. The room, with all its lights, seemed strange, and there were shadows behind everything. Then the woman yelled again, just noise this time. Either a person is fearless, Peter thought coldly, or he isn't fearless. He started walking slowly toward the front door. There was a long mirror in the foyer and he got a good look at himself. His arms looked very thin.

The woman began hammering once more on the front door and Peter looked at it closely. It was a big steel door, but it was shaking minutely, as though somebody with a machine was working on it. For the first time he heard another voice. It was a man's voice, only it didn't sound quite like a man's voice. It sounded like an animal in a cave, growling and deciding to do something unreasonable. In all the scenes of threat and violence on the television set, Peter had never heard anything at all like it. He moved slowly toward the door, feeling the way he had felt when he had the flu, remembering how thin his arms looked in the mirror, regretting that he had decided to be fearless.

11

"Oh, God!" the woman yelled, "Oh, God, don't do it!"

Then there was some more hammering and the low, animal sound of the beast in the cave that you never heard over the air, and he threw the door open.

Mrs. Chalmers was there in the vestibule, on her knees, facing him, and behind her Mr. Chalmers was standing, leaning against the wall, with the door to his own apartment open behind him. Mr. Chalmers was making that funny sound and he had a gun in his hand and he was pointing it at Mrs. Chalmers.

The vestibule was small and it had what Peter's mother called Early American wallpaper and a brass light fixture. There were only the two doors opening on the vestibule, and the Chalmers had a mat in front of theirs with "Welcome" written on it. The Chalmers were in their mid-thirties, and Peter's mother always said about them, "One thing about our neighbors, they *are* quiet." She also said that Mrs. Chalmers put a lot of money on her back.

Mrs. Chalmers was kind of fat and her hair was pretty blond and her complexion was soft and pink and she always looked as though she had been in the beauty parlor all afternoon. She always said, "My, you're getting to be a big boy" to Peter when she met him in the elevator, in a soft voice, as though she was just about to laugh. She must have said that fifty times by now. She had a good, strong smell of perfume on her all the time, too.

Mr. Chalmers wore pince-nez glasses most of the time and he was getting bald and he worked late at his office a good many evenings of the week. When he met Peter in the elevator he would say, "It's getting colder," or "It's getting warmer," and that was all, so Peter had no opinion about him, except that he looked like the principal of a school.

But now Mrs. Chalmers was on her knees in the vestibule

and her dress was torn and she was crying and there were black streaks on her cheeks and she didn't look as though she'd just come from the beauty parlor. And Mr. Chalmers wasn't wearing a jacket and he didn't have his glasses on and what hair he had was mussed all over his head and he was leaning against the Early American wallpaper making this animal noise, and he had a big, heavy pistol in his hand and he was pointing it right at Mrs. Chalmers.

"Let me in!" Mrs. Chalmers yelled, still on her knees. "You've got to let me in. He's going to kill me. *Please!*"

"Mrs. Chalmers . . ." Peter began. His voice sounded as though he were trying to talk under water, and it was very hard to say the *s* at the end of her name. He put out his hands uncertainly in front of him, as though he expected somebody to throw him something.

"Get inside, you," Mr. Chalmers said.

Peter looked at Mr. Chalmers. He was only five feet away and without his glasses he was squinting. Peter feinted with his eyes, or at least later in his life he thought he had feinted with his eyes. Mr. Chalmers didn't do anything. He just stood there, with the pistol pointed, somehow, it seemed to Peter, at both Mrs. Chalmers and himself at the same time. Five feet was a long distance, a long, long distance.

"Good night," Peter said, and he closed the door.

There was a single sob on the other side of the door and that was all.

Peter went in and put the uneaten grapes back in the refrigerator, flicking on the light as he went into the kitchen and leaving it on when he went out. Then he went back to the living room and got the stems from the first bunch of grapes and threw them into the fireplace, because otherwise his mother would notice and look for the seeds and not see them and give him four tablespoons of milk of magnesia the next day.

Then, leaving the lights on in the living room, although he knew what his mother would say about that when she got home, he went into his room and quickly got into bed. He waited for the sound of shots. There were two or three noises that might have been shots, but in the city it was hard to tell.

He was still awake when his parents came home. He heard his mother's voice, and he knew from the sound she was complaining about the lights in the living room and kitchen, but he pretended to be sleeping when she came into his room to look at him. He didn't want to start in with his mother about the Chalmers, because then she'd ask when it had happened and she'd want to know what he was doing up at twelve o'clock.

He kept listening for shots for a long time, and he got hot and damp under the covers and then freezing cold. He heard several sharp, ambiguous noises in the quiet night, but nothing that you could be sure about, and after a while he fell asleep.

In the morning, Peter got out of bed early, dressed quickly, and went silently out of the apartment without waking his parents. The vestibule looked just the way it always did, with the brass lamp and the flowered wallpaper and the Chalmers' doormat with "Welcome" on it. There were no bodies and no blood. Sometimes when Mrs. Chalmers had been standing there waiting for the elevator, you could smell her perfume for a long time after. But now there was no smell of perfume, just the dusty, apartment house usual smell. Peter stared at the Chalmers' door nervously while waiting for the elevator to come up, but it didn't open and no sound came from within.

Sam, the man who ran the elevator and who didn't like him, anyway, only grunted when Peter got into the elevator, and Peter decided not to ask him any questions. He went out into the chilly, bright Sunday morning street, half expecting to see the morgue wagon in front of the door, or at least two or three prowl cars. But there was only a sleepy woman in slacks airing a boxer and a man with his collar turned up hurrying up from the corner with the newspapers under his arm.

Peter went across the street and looked up to the sixth floor, at the windows of the Chalmers' apartment. The Venetian blinds were pulled shut in every room and all the windows were closed.

A policeman walked down the other side of the street, heavy, blue, and purposeful, and for a moment Peter felt close to arrest. But the policeman continued on toward the avenue and turned the corner and disappeared and Peter said to himself, "They never know anything."

He walked up and down the street, first on one side, then on the other, waiting, although it was hard to know what he was waiting for. He saw a hand come out through the blinds in his parents' room and slam the window shut, and he knew he ought to get upstairs quickly with a good excuse for being out, but he couldn't face them this morning, and he would invent an excuse later. Maybe he would even say he had gone to the museum, although he doubted that his mother would swallow that. Some excuse. Later.

Then, after he had been patrolling the street for almost two hours, the door opened and Mr. and Mrs. Chalmers came out. He had on his pince-nez and a dark-gray hat, and

Mrs. Chalmers had on her fur coat and a red hat with feathers on it. Mr. Chalmers was holding the door open politely for his wife, and she looked, as she came out the door, as though she had just come from the beauty parlor.

It was too late to turn back or avoid them, and Peter just stood still, five feet from the entrance.

"Good morning," Mr. Chalmers said as he took his wife's arm and they started walking past Peter.

"Good morning, Peter," said Mrs. Chalmers in her soft voice, smiling at him. "Isn't it a nice day today?"

"Good morning," Peter said, and he was surprised that it came out and sounded like good morning.

The Chalmers walked down the street toward Madison Avenue, two married people, arm in arm, going to church or to a big hotel for Sunday breakfast. Peter watched them, ashamed. He was ashamed of Mrs. Chalmers for looking the way she did the night before, down on her knees, and yelling like that and being so afraid. He was ashamed of Mr. Chalmers for making the noise that was not like the noise of a human being, and for threatening to shoot Mrs. Chalmers and not doing it. And he was ashamed of himself because he had been fearless when he opened the door, but had not been fearless ten seconds later, with Mr. Chalmers five feet away with the gun. He was ashamed of himself for not taking Mrs. Chalmers into the apartment, ashamed because he was not lying now with a bullet in his heart. But most of all he was ashamed because they had all said good morning to each other and the Chalmers were walking quietly together, arm in arm, in the windy sunlight, toward Madison Avenue.

It was nearly eleven o'clock when Peter got back to the apartment, but his parents had gone back to sleep. There was a pretty good program on at eleven, about counterspies in Asia, and he turned it on automatically, while eating an orange. It was pretty exciting, but then there was a part in which an Oriental held a ticking bomb in his hand in a roomful of Americans, and Peter could tell what was coming. The hero, who was fearless and who came from California, was beginning to feint with his eyes, and Peter reached over and turned the set off. It closed down with a shivering, collapsing pattern. Blinking a little, Peter watched the blind screen for a moment.

Ah, he thought in sudden, permanent disbelief, after the night in which he had faced the incomprehensible, shameless, weaponed grown-up world and had failed to disarm it, ah, they can have that, that's for kids.

RUTH RENDELL

The Vinegar
Mother

All this happened when I was eleven.

Mop Felton was at school with me and she was supposed to be my friend. I say "supposed to be" because she was one of those close friends all little girls seem
to have yet don't very much like. I had never liked Mop. I
knew it then just as I know it now, but she was my friend
because she lived in the next street, was the same age, in the
same grade, and because my parents, though not particularly intimate with the Feltons, would have it so.

Mop was a nervous, strained, dramatic creature, in some
ways old for her age and in others very young. Hindsight
tells me that she had no self-confidence but much self-
esteem. She was an only child who flew into noisy rages or
silent huffs when teased. She was tall and very skinny and
dark, and it wasn't her hair, thin and lank, which accounted
for her nickname. Her proper name was Alicia. I don't
know why we called her Mop, and if now I see in it some

18

obscure allusion to mopping and mowing (a Shakespearean description which might have been associated with her) or in the monosyllable the hint of a witch's familiar (again, not inept), I am attributing to us an intellectual sophistication which we didn't possess.

We were gluttons for nicknames. Perhaps all schoolgirls are. But there was neither subtlety nor finesse in our selection. Margaret myself, I was dubbed Margarine. Rhoda Joseph, owing to some gagging and embarrassment during a public recitation of Wordsworth, was forever after Lucy; Elizabeth Goodwin was Goat because this epithet had once been applied to her by higher authority on the hockey field. Our nicknames were not exclusive, being readily interchangeable with our true Christian names at will. We never used them in the presence of parent or teacher and they, if they had known of them, would not have deigned use them to us. It was, therefore, all the more astonishing to hear them from the lips of Mr. Felton, the oldest and richest of any of our fathers.

Coming home from work into a room where Mop and I were, "How's my old Mopsy, then?" he would say, and to me, "Well, it's jolly old Margarine!"

I used to giggle, as I always did when confronted by something mildly embarrassing that I didn't understand. I was an observant child, but not sensitive. Children, in any case, are little given to empathy. I can't recall that I ever pitied Mop for having a father who, though over fifty, pretended too often to be her contemporary. But I found it satisfactory that my own father, at her entry, would look up vaguely from his book and mutter, "Hello—er, Alicia, isn't it?"

The Feltons were on a slightly higher social plane than

we, a fact I did know and accepted without question and without resentment. Their house was bigger, each parent possessed a car, they ate dinner in the evenings. Mr. Felton used to give Mop half a glass of sherry to drink.

"I don't want you growing up ignorant of wine," he would say.

And if I were present I would get the sherry, too. I suppose it was Manzanilla, for it was very dry and pale yellow, the color of the stone in a ring Mrs. Felton wore which entirely hid her wedding ring.

They had a cottage in the country where they went at the weekends and sometimes for the summer holidays. Once they took me there for a day. And the summer after my eleventh birthday, Mr. Felton said, "Why don't you take old Margarine with you for the holidays?"

It seems strange now that I should have wanted to go. I had a very happy childhood, a calm, unthinking, unchanging relationship with my parents and my brothers. I liked Rhoda and Elizabeth far more than I liked Mop, whose rages and fantasies and sulks annoyed me, and I disliked Mrs. Felton more than any grown-up I knew. Yet I did want to go very much. The truth was that even then I had begun to develop my passion for houses, the passion that has led me to become a designer of them, and one day in that cottage had been enough to make me love it. All my life had been spent in a semi-detached villa, circa 1935, in a London suburb. The Feltons' cottage, which had the pretentious (not to me, then) name of Sanctuary, was four hundred years old, thatched, half-timbered, of wattle and daub construction, a calendar-maker's dream, a chocolate-box artist's ideal. I wanted to sleep within those ancient walls, tread upon floors that had been there before the Armada came, press my face against glass panes that had reflected a ruff or a Puritan's starched collar.

My mother put up a little opposition. She liked me to know Mop, she also perhaps liked me to be associated with the Feltons' social cachet, but I had noticed before that she didn't much like me to be in the care of Mrs. Felton.

"And Mr. Felton will only be there at the weekends," she said.

"If Margaret doesn't like it," said my father, "she can write home and get us to send her a telegram saying you've broken your leg."

"Thanks very much," said my mother. "I wish you wouldn't teach the children habits of deception."

But in the end she agreed. If I were unhappy, I was to phone from the call box in the village and then they would write and say my grandmother wanted me to go and stay with her. Which, apparently, was not teaching me habits of deception.

In the event, I wasn't at all unhappy, and it was to be a while before I was even disquieted. There was plenty to do. It was fruit-growing country, and Mop and I picked fruit for Mr. Gould, the farmer. We got paid for this, which Mrs. Felton seemed to think *infra dig*. She didn't associate with the farmers or the agricultural workers. Her greatest friend was a certain Lady Elsworthy, an old woman whose title (I later learned she was the widow of a Civil Service knight) placed her in my estimation in the forefront of the aristocracy. I was stricken dumb whenever she and her son were at Sanctuary and much preferred the company of our nearest neighbor, a Mrs. Potter, who was perhaps gratified to meet a juvenile enthusiast of architecture. Anyway, she secured for me the entrée to the Hall, a William and Mary mansion, through whose vast chambers I walked hand in hand with her, awed and wondering and very well content.

Sanctuary had a small parlor, a large dining-living room, a kitchen, and a bathroom on the ground floor and two bedrooms upstairs. The ceilings were low and sloping and so excessively beamed, some of the beams being carved, that were I to see it now I would probably think it vulgar, though knowing it authentic. I am sure that nowadays I would think the Feltons' furniture vulgar, for their wealth, such as it was, didn't run to the purchasing of true antiques. Instead, they had those piecrust tables and rent tables and little escritoires which, cunningly chipped and scratched in the right places, inlaid with convincingly scuffed and dimly gilded leather—maroon, olive, or amber—had been manufactured at a factory in Romford.

I knew this because Mr. Felton, down for the weekend, would announce it to whomsoever might be present.

"And how old do you suppose that is, Lady Elsworthy?" he would say, fingering one of those deceitful little tables as he placed on it her glass of citrine-colored sherry. "A hundred and fifty years? Two hundred?"

Of course she didn't know or was too well-bred to say.

"One year's your answer! Factory-made last year and I defy anyone but an expert to tell the difference."

Then Mop would have her half-glass of sherry and I mine while the adults watched us for the signs of intoxication they seemed to find so amusing in the young and so disgraceful in the old. And then dinner with red or white wine, but none for us this time. They always had wine, even when, as was often the case, the meal was only sandwiches or bits of cold stuff on toast. Mr. Felton used to bring it down with him on Saturdays, a dozen bottles sometimes in a cardboard case. I wonder if it was good French wine or sour cheap stuff from Algeria that my father called plonk? Whatever Mr. Felton's indulgence with the sherry had taught me, it was not to lose my ignorance of wine.

But wine plays a part in this story, an important part. For, as she sipped the dark red stuff in her glass, blood-black with—or am I imagining this?—a blacker scaling of lees in its depths, Lady Elsworthy said, "Even if you're only a moderate wine drinker, my dear, you ought, you really ought, to have a vinegar mother."

On this occasion I wasn't the only person present to giggle. There were cries of "A *what?*" and some laughter and then Lady Elsworthy began an explanation of what a vinegar mother was, a culture of acetobacter that would convert wine into vinegar. Her son, whom the adults called Peter, supplied the technical details and the Potters asked questions and from time to time someone would say, "A vinegar mother! What a name!" I wasn't much interested and I wandered off into the garden, where, after a few minutes, Mop joined me. She was, as usual, carrying a book but instead of sitting down, opening the book and excluding me, which was her custom, she stood staring into the distance of the Stour Valley and the Weeping Hills—I think she leaned against a tree—and her face had on it that protuberant-featured expression which heralded one of her rages. I asked her what was the matter.

"I've been sick."

I knew she hadn't been, but I asked her why.

"That horrible old woman and that horrible thing she was talking about, like a bit of liver in a bottle, she said." Her mouth trembled. "Why does she call it a vinegar *mother?*"

"I don't know," I said. "Perhaps because mothers make children and it makes vinegar."

That only seemed to make her angrier and she kicked at the tree.

"Shall we go down to the pond or are you going to read?" I said.

But Mop didn't answer me so I went down to the pond alone and watched the bats that flitted against a pale green sky. Mop had gone up to our bedroom. She was in bed reading when I got back. No reader myself, I remember the books she liked and remember too that my mother thought she ought not to be allowed to read them. That night it was Lefanu's *Uncle Silas* which engrossed her. She had just finished Dr. James's *Ghost Stories of an Antiquary*. I don't believe, at that time, I saw any connection between her literary tastes and her reaction to the vinegar mother, nor did I attribute this latter to anything lacking in her relationship with her own mother. I couldn't have done so; I was much too young. I hadn't, anyway, been affected by the conversation at supper and I went to bed with no uneasy forebodings about what was to come.

In the morning when Mop and I came back from church—we were sent there, I now think, from a desire on the part of Mr. and Mrs. Felton to impress the neighbors rather than out of vicarious piety—we found the Elsworthys once more at Sanctuary. Lady Elsworthy and her son and Mrs. Felton were all peering into a glass vessel with a narrow, stoppered mouth in which was some brown liquid with a curd floating on it. This curd did look quite a lot like a slice of liver.

"It's alive," said Mop. "It's a sort of animal."

Lady Elsworthy told her not to be a little fool and Mrs.

Felton laughed. I thought my mother would have been angry if a visitor to our house had told me not to be a fool, and I also thought Mop was really going to be sick this time.

"We don't have to have it, do we?" she said.

"Of course we're going to have it," said Mrs. Felton. "How dare you speak like that when Lady Elsworthy has been kind enough to give it to me! Now we shall never have to buy nasty shop vinegar again."

"Vinegar doesn't cost much," said Mop.

"Isn't that just like a child! Money grows on trees as far as she's concerned."

Then Lady Elsworthy started giving instructions for the maintenance of the thing. It must be kept in a warm atmosphere. "Not out in your chilly kitchen, my dear." It was to be fed with wine, the dregs of each bottle they consumed. "But not white wine. You tell her why not, Peter; you know I'm no good at the scientific stuff." It must never be touched with a knife or metal spoon.

"If metal touches it," said Peter Elsworthy, "it will shrivel and die. In some ways, you see, it's a tender plant."

Mop had banged out of the room. Lady Elsworthy was once more bent over her gift, holding the vessel and placing it in a suitable position where it was neither too light nor too cold. From the garden I could hear the drone of the lawn mower, plied by Mr. Felton. Those other two had moved a little away from the window, away from the broad shaft of sunshine in which we had found them bathed. As Peter Elsworthy spoke of the tender plant, I saw his eyes meet Mrs. Felton's and there passed between them a glance, mysterious, beyond my comprehension, years away from anything I knew. His face became soft and strange. I wanted to

giggle as I sometimes giggled in the cinema, but I knew better than to do so there, and I went away and giggled by
myself in the garden, saying, "Soppy, soppy!" and kicking at
a stone.

But I wasn't alone. Mr. Felton came pushing the lawn
mower up behind me. He used to sweat in the heat and his
face was red and wet like the middle of a joint of beef when
the brown part has been carved off. A grandfather rather
than a father, I thought him.

"What's soppy, my old Margarine? Mind out of my way or
I'll cut your tail off."

It was August and the season had begun, so on Sunday
afternoons he would take the shotgun he kept hanging in
the kitchen and go out after rabbits. I believe he did this less
from a desire to eat rabbit flesh than from a need to keep in
with the Elsworthys, who shot every unprotected thing that
flew or scuttled. But he was a poor shot and I used to feel
relieved when he came back empty-handed. On Sunday
evenings he drove away to London.

"Poor old Daddy back to the grindstone," he would say.
"Take care of yourself, my old Mop." And to me, with wit,
"Don't melt away in all this sunshine, Margarine."

That Sunday Mrs. Felton made him promise to bring a
dozen more bottles of wine when he returned the following
weekend.

"Reinforcements for my vinegar mother."

"It's stupid wasting wine to make it into vinegar," said
Mop. I wondered why she used to hover so nervously about
her parents at this leave-taking time, watching them both,
her fists clenched. Now I know it was because, although she
was rude to them and seemed not to care for them, she
longed desperately to see them exchange some demonstra-

tion of affection greater than Mrs. Felton's apathetic lifting of her cheek and the hungry peck Mr. Felton deposited upon it. But she waited in vain, and when the car had gone would burst into a seemingly inexplicable display of ill-temper or sulks.

So another week began, a week in which our habits, until then routine and placid, were to change.

Like a proper writer, a professional, I have hinted at Mrs. Felton and, I hope, whetted appetites, but I have delayed till now giving any description of her. But, having announced her entry through the mouths of my characters (as in all the best plays), I shall delay no more. The stage is ready for her and she shall enter it, in her robes and with her trumpets.

She was a tall, thin woman and her skin was as brown as a pale Indian's. I thought her old and very ugly, and I couldn't understand a remark of my mother's that I had overheard to the effect that Mrs. Felton was "quite beautiful if you like that gypsy look." I suppose she was about thirty-seven or thirty-eight. Her hair was black and frizzy, like a bush of heather singed by fire, and it grew so low on her forehead that her black brows sprang up to meet it, leaving only an inch or so of skin between. She had a big mouth with brown thick lips she never painted and enormous eyes whose whites were like wet eggshells.

In the country she wore slacks and a shirt. She made some of her own clothes and those she made were dramatic. I remember a hooded cloak she had of brown hessian and a long evening gown of embroidered linen. At that time women seldom wore cloaks or long dresses, either for eve-

27

ning or day. She chain-smoked and her fingers were yellow with nicotine.

Me she almost entirely ignored. I was fed and made to wash properly and told to change my clothes and not allowed to be out after dark. But apart from this she hardly spoke to me. I think she had a ferocious dislike of children, for Mop fared very little better than I did. Mrs. Felton was one of those women who fall into the habit of only addressing their children to scold them. However presentable Mop might make herself, however concentratedly good on occasion her behavior—for I believe she made great efforts—Mrs. Felton couldn't bring herself to praise. Or if she could, there would always be the sting in the tail, the "Well, but look at your nails!" or "It's very nice but do you have to pick this moment?" And Mop's name on her tongue—as if specifically chosen to this end—rang with a sour slither, a little green snake slipping from its hole, as the liquid and the sibilant scathed out, "Alicia!"

But at the beginning of that third week a slight change came upon her. She was not so much nicer or kinder as more vague, more nervously abstracted. Mop's peccadillos passed unnoticed and I, if late for a meal received no venomous glance. It was on the Tuesday evening that the first wine bottle appeared at our supper table.

We ate this meal, cold usually but more than a bread and butter tea, at half past seven or eight in the evening, and after it we were sent to bed. There had never before been the suggestion that we should take wine with it. Even at the weekends we were never given wine, apart from our tiny glasses of educative sherry. But that night at sunset—I remember the room all orange and quiet and warm—Mrs. Felton brought to the table a bottle of red wine instead of the teapot and the lemon barley water, and set out three glasses.

"I don't like wine," said Mop.

"Yes, you do. You like sherry."

"I don't like that dark red stuff. It tastes bitter. Daddy won't let me have wine."

"Then we won't tell Daddy. If it's bitter you can put sugar in it. My God, any other child would think it was in heaven getting wine for supper. You don't know when you're well off and you never have. You've no appreciation."

"I suppose you want us to drink it so you can have the leftovers for your horrible vinegar thing," said Mop.

"It's not horrible and don't you dare to speak to me like that," said Mrs. Felton, but there was something like relief in her voice. Can I remember that? Did I truly observe *that*? No. It is now that I know it, now when all the years have passed, and year by year has come more understanding. Then, I heard no relief. I saw no baser motive in Mrs. Felton's insistence. I took it for granted, absurd and somehow an inversion of the proper course of things though it seemed, that we were to drink an expensive substance in order that the remains of it might be converted into a cheap substance. But childhood is a looking-glass country where so often one is obliged to believe six impossible things before breakfast.

I drank my wine and, grudgingly, Mop drank two full glasses into which she had stirred sugar. Most of the rest was consumed by Mrs. Felton, who then poured the dregs into the glass vessel for the refreshment of the vinegar mother. I don't think I had ever drunk or even tasted table wine before. It went to my head, and as soon as I was in bed at nine o'clock I fell into a profound thick sleep.

But Mop was asleep before me. She had lurched into bed without washing and I heard her heavy breathing while I was pulling on my nightdress. This was unusual. Mop wasn't exactly an insomniac but, for a child, she was a bad sleeper. Most evenings as I was passing into those soft clouds of sleep, into a delightful drowsiness that at any moment would be closed off by total oblivion, I would hear her toss and turn in bed or even get up and move about the room. I knew, too, that sometimes she went downstairs for a glass of water or perhaps just for her mother's company, for on the mornings after such excursions Mrs. Felton would take her to task over breakfast, scathingly demanding of invisible hearers why she should have been cursed with such a restless, nervy child, who, even as a baby, had never slept a peaceful night through.

On the Tuesday night, however, she had no difficulty in falling asleep. It was later, in the depths of the night (as she told me in the morning) that she had awakened and lain wakeful for hours, or so she said. She had heard the church clock chime two and three; her head had ached and she had had a curious trembling in her limbs. But, as far as I know, she said nothing of this to her mother, and her headache must have passed by the middle of the morning. For, when I left the house at ten to go with Mrs. Potter to an auction that was being held in some neighboring mansion, she was lying on a blanket on the front lawn, reading the book Mr. Felton had brought down for her at the weekend, *Fifty Haunted Houses*. And she was still reading it, was deep in "The Mezzotint" or some horror of Blackwood's, when I got back at one.

It must have been that day, too, when she began to get what I should now call obsessional about the vinegar mother. Several times, three or four times certainly, when I went into the dining room, I found her standing by the Romford factory antique on which Lady Elsworthy's present stood, gazing with the fascination of someone who views an encapsulated reptile, at the culture within. It was not to me in any way noisome or sinister, nor was it even particularly novel. I had seen a dish of stewed fruit forgotten and allowed to ferment in my grandmother's larder, and apart from the fungus on that being pale green, there was little difference between it and this crust of bacteria. Mop's face, so repelled yet so compelled, made me giggle. A mistake, this, for she turned on me, lashing out with a thin wiry arm.

"Shut up, shut up! I hate you."

But she had calmed and was speaking to me again by suppertime. We sat on the wall above the road and watched Mr. Gould's Herefords driven from their pasture up the lane home to the farm. Swallows perched on the telephone wires like taut strings of black and white beads. The sky was lemony-green and greater birds flew homeward across it.

"I'd like to put a spoon in it," said Mop, "and then I'd see it shrivel up and die."

"She'd know," I said.

"Who's she?"

"Your mother, of course." I was surprised at the question when the answer was so obvious. "Who else?"

"I don't know."

"It's only an old fungus," I said. "It isn't hurting you."

"Alicia! Aleeciah!" A sharp liquid cry, the sound of a sight, and the sight wine or vinegar flung in a curving jet.

"Come on, Margarine," said Mop. "Supper's ready."

We were given no wine that night, but on the next a bottle and the glasses once more appeared. The meal was a heavier one than usual, meat pie with potatoes as well as salad. Perhaps the wine was sweet this time or of a finer vintage, for it tasted good to me and I drank two glasses. It never occurred to me to wonder what my parents, moderate and very nearly abstemious, would have thought of this corruption of their daughter. Of course it didn't. To a child grown-ups are omniscient and all-wise. Much as I disliked Mrs. Felton, I never supposed she could wish to harm me or be indifferent as to whether or not I were harmed.

Mop, too, obeyed and drank. This time there was no demur from her. Probably she was once again trying methods of ingratiation. We went to bed at nine and I think Mop went to sleep before me. I slept heavily as usual, but I was aware of some disturbance in the night, of having been briefly awakened and spoken to. I remembered this, though not much more for a while, when I finally woke in the morning. It was about seven, a pearly morning of birdsong, and Mop was sitting on the window seat in her nightdress.

She looked awful, as if she had got a bad cold coming or had just been sick.

"I tried to wake you up in the night," she said.

"I thought you had," I said. "Did you have a dream?"

She shook her head. "I woke up and I heard the clock strike one and then I heard footsteps on the path down there."

"In this garden, d'you mean?" I said. "Going or coming?"

"I don't know," she said oddly. "They must have been coming."

"It was a burglar," I said. "We ought to go down and see if things have been stolen."

"It wasn't a burglar." Mop was getting angry with me and her face was blotchy. "I did go down. I lay awake for a bit and I didn't hear any more, but I couldn't go back to sleep and I wanted a drink of water. So I went down."

"Well, go on," I said.

But Mop couldn't go on. And even I, insensitive and unsympathetic to her as I was, could see she had been badly frightened, was still frightened, and then I remembered what had wakened me in the night, exactly what had happened. I remembered being brought to brief consciousness by the choking gasps of someone who is screaming in her sleep. Mop had screamed herself awake and the words she had spoken to me had been, "The vinegar mother! The vinegar mother!"

"You had a nightmare," I said.

"Oh, shut up," said Mop. "You never listen. I shan't ever tell you anything again."

But later in the day she did tell me. I think that by this time she had got it into some sort of proportion, although she was still very frightened when she got to the climax of what she insisted couldn't have been a dream. She had, she said, gone downstairs about half an hour after she heard the footsteps in the garden. She hadn't put a light on, as the moon was bright. The dining room door was partly open, and when she looked inside she saw a hooded figure crouched in a chair by the window. The figure was all in brown, and Mop said she saw the hood slide back and disclose its face. The thing that had made her scream and scream was this face which wasn't a face at all, but a shapeless mass of liver.

"You dreamed it," I said. "You must have. You were in bed when you screamed, so you must have been dreaming."

"I did go down," Mop insisted.

"Maybe you did," I said, "but the other bit was a dream.

33

Your mother would have come if she'd heard you scream-ing downstairs."

No more was said about the dream or whatever it was after that, and on Saturday Mr. Felton arrived and took us to the Young Farmers' Show at Marks Tey. He brought me my parents' love and the news that my eldest brother had passed his exam and got seven O Levels, and I was happy. He went shooting with Peter Elsworthy on Sunday after-noon, and Peter came back with him and promised to drive me and Mop and Mrs. Felton to the seaside for the day on Tuesday.

It was a beautiful day that Tuesday, perhaps the best of all the days at Sanctuary, and I, who, on the morning after Mop's dream, had begun to wonder about making that de-ceitful phone call from the village, felt I could happily re-main till term began. We took a picnic lunch and swam in the wide shallow sea. Mrs. Felton wore a proper dress of blue and white cotton which made her brown skin look like a tan, and had smoothed down her hair, and smiled and was gracious and once called Mop dear. Suddenly I liked Peter Elsworthy. I suppose I had one of those infatuations for him that are fused in young girls by a kind smile, one sentence spoken as to a contemporary, one casual touch of the hand. On that sunny beach I was moved toward him by inexplicable feelings, moved into a passion the sight of him had never before inspired, which was to die as quickly as it had been born when the sun had gone, the sea was left be-hind, and he was once more Mrs. Felton's friend in the front seats of the car.

I had followed him about that day like a little dog, and perhaps it was my unconcealed devotion that drove him to leave us at our gate and refuse even to come in and view the

progress of the vinegar mother. His excuse was that he had
to accompany his mother to an aunt's for dinner. Mrs. Felton sulked ferociously after he had gone and we got a supper of runny scrambled eggs and lemon barley water.

On the following night there appeared on our table a bottle of claret. The phone rang while we were eating, and
while Mrs. Felton was away answering it I took the daring
step of pouring my wine into the vinegar mother.

"I shall tell her," said Mop.

"I don't care," I said. "I can't drink it, nasty, sour, horrible stuff."

"You shouldn't call my father's wine horrible when you're
a guest," said Mop, but she didn't tell Mrs. Felton. I think
she would have poured her own to follow mine except that
she was afraid the level in the vessel would rise too much, or
was it that by then nothing would have induced her to come
within feet of the culture?

I didn't need wine to make me sleep, but if I had taken it
I might have slept more heavily. A thin moonlight was in
the room when I woke up to see Mop's bed empty. Mop was
standing by the door, holding it half open, and she was
trembling. It was a bit eerie in there with Mop's long
shadow jumping about against the zigzag beams on the wall.
But I couldn't hear a sound.

"What's the matter now?" I said.

"There's someone down there."

"How d'you know? Is there a light on?"

"I heard glass," she said.

How can you hear glass? But I knew what she meant and
I didn't much like it. I got up and went over to the doorway
and looked down the stairs. There was light coming from
under the dining room door, a white glow that could have

been from the moon or from the oil lamp they sometimes used. Then I too heard glass, a chatter of glass against glass and a thin trickling sound.

Mop said in a breathy, hysterical voice, "Suppose she goes about in the night to every place where they've got one? She goes about and watches over them and makes it happen. She's down there now doing it. Listen!"

Glass against glass. . . .

"That's crazy," I said. "It's those books you read."

She didn't say anything. We closed the door and lay in our bed with the bedlamp on. The light made it better. We heard the clock strike twelve. I said, "Can we go to sleep now?" And when Mop nodded I put out the light.

The moon had gone away, covered perhaps by clouds. Into the black silence came a curious drawn-out cry. I know now what it was, but no child of eleven could know. I was only aware then that it was no cry of grief or pain or terror, but of triumph, of something at last attained; yet it was at the same time inhuman, utterly outside the bonds of human restraint.

Mop began to scream.

I had the light on and was jumping up and down on my bed, shouting to her to stop, when the door was flung open and Mrs. Felton came in, her hair a wild heathery mass, a dressing gown of quilted silk, black-blood color, wrapped around her and tied at the waist with savagery. Rage and violence were what I expected. But Mrs. Felton said nothing. She did what I had never seen her do, had never supposed anything would make her do. She caught Mop in an embrace and hugged her, rocking her back and forth. They were both crying, swaying on the bed and crying. I heard footsteps on the garden path, soft, stealthy, finally fading away.

Mop said nothing at all about it to me the next day. She withdrew into her books and sulks. I believe now that the isolated demonstration of affection she had received from her mother in the night led her to hope more might follow. But Mrs. Felton had become weirdly reserved, as if in some sort of long dream. I noticed with giggly embarrassment that she hardly seemed to see Mop hanging about her, looking into her face, trying to get her attention. When Mop gave up at last and took refuge in the garden with Dr. James on demons, Mrs. Felton lay on the dining room sofa, smoking and staring at the ceiling. I went in once to fetch my cardigan—for Mrs. Potter was taking me to the medieval town at Lavenham for the afternoon—and she was still lying there, smiling strangely to herself, her long brown hands playing with her necklace of reddish-brown beads.

She went off for a walk by herself on Friday afternoon and she was gone for hours. It was very hot, too hot to be in a garden with only thin apple tree shade. I was sitting at the dining room table, working on a scrapbook of country house pictures Mrs. Potter had got me to make, and Mop was reading, when the phone rang. Mop answered it, but from the room where I was, across the passage, I could hear Mr. Felton's hearty bray.

"How's life treating you, my old Mop?"

I heard it all, how he was coming down that night instead of in the morning and would be here by midnight. She might pass the message on to her mother, but not to worry as he had his own key. And his kind regards to jolly old Margarine if she hadn't, by this time, melted away into a little puddle!

Mrs. Felton came back at five in Peter Elsworthy's car. There were leaves in her hair and bits of grass on the back of her skirt. They pored over the vinegar mother, moving it back into a cool, dark corner, and enthusing over the color of the liquor under the floating liver-like mass.

"A tender plant that mustn't get overheated," said Peter Elsworthy, picking a leaf out of Mrs. Felton's hair and laughing. I wondered why I had ever liked him or thought him kind.

Mop and I were given rosé with our supper out of a dumpy little bottle with a picture of cloisters on its label. By now Mrs. Felton must have learned that I didn't need wine to make me sleep, so she didn't insist on my having more than one glass. The vinegar mother's vessel was three-quarters full.

I was in bed and Mop nearly undressed when I remembered about her father's message.

"I forgot to tell her," said Mop, yawning and heavy-eyed.

"You could go down and tell her now."

"She'd be cross. Besides, he's got his key."

"You don't like going down in the dark by yourself," I said. Mop didn't answer. She got into bed and pulled the sheet over her head.

We never spoke to each other again.

She didn't return to school that term, and at the end of it my mother told me she wasn't coming back. I never learned what happened to her. The last—almost the last—I remember of her was her thin sallow face that lately had always looked bewildered, and the dark circles around her old-woman's eyes. I remember the books on the bedside table: *Fifty Haunted Houses*, the *Works of Sheridan Lefanu*, *The Best of Montague Rhodes James*. The pale lacquering of moonlight in that room with its beams and its slanted ceiling. The silence of night in an old and haunted countryside. Wine breath in my throat and wine weariness bringing heavy sleep. . . .

Out of that thick slumber I was awakened by two sharp explosions and the sound of breaking glass. Mop had gone from the bedroom before I was out of bed, scarcely aware of where I was, my head swimming. Somewhere downstairs Mop was screaming. I went down. The whole house, the house called Sanctuary, was bright with lights. I opened the dining room door.

Mr. Felton was leaning against the table, the shotgun still in his hand. I think he was crying. I don't remember much blood, only the brown, dead nakedness of Mrs. Felton spread on the floor, with Peter Elsworthy bent over her, holding his wounded arm. And the smell of gunpowder like fireworks and the stronger sickening stench of vinegar everywhere, and broken glass in shards, and Mop screaming, plunging a knife again and again into a thick, slimy liver mass on the carpet.

STANLEY ELLIN

Robert

The windows of the Sixth Grade classroom were wide open to the June afternoon, and through them came all the sounds of the departing school: the thunder of bus motors warming up, the hiss of gravel under running feet, the voices raised in cynical fervor.

> "So we sing all hail to thee,
> District Schoo-wull Number Three . . ."

Miss Gildea flinched a little at the last high, shrill note, and pressed her fingers to her aching forehead. She was tired, more tired than she could ever recall being in her thirty-eight years of teaching, and, as she told herself, she had reason to be. It had not been a good term, not good at all, what with the size of the class, and the Principal's insistence on new methods, and then her mother's shocking death coming right in the middle of everything.

Perhaps she had been too close to her mother, Miss

Gildea thought; perhaps she had been wrong, never taking into account that some day the old lady would have to pass on and leave her alone in the world. Well, thinking about it all the time didn't make it easier. She should try to forget.

And, of course, to add to her troubles, there had been during the past few weeks this maddening business of Robert. He had been a perfectly nice boy, and then, out of a clear sky, had become impossible. Not bothersome or noisy really, but sunk into an endless daydream from which Miss Gildea had to sharply jar him a dozen times a day.

She turned her attention to Robert, who sat alone in the room at the desk immediately before her, a thin boy with neatly combed, colorless hair bracketed between large ears; mild blue eyes in a pale face fixed solemnly on hers.

"Robert."

"Yes, Miss Gildea."

"Do you know why I told you to remain after school, Robert?"

He frowned thoughtfully at this, as if it were some lesson he was being called on for, but had failed to memorize properly.

"I suppose for being bad," he said, at last.

Miss Gildea sighed.

"No, Robert, that's not it at all. I know a bad boy when I see one, Robert, and you aren't one like that. But I do know there's something troubling you, something on your mind, and I think I can help you."

"There's nothing bothering me, Miss Gildea. Honest, there isn't."

Miss Gildea found the silver pencil thrust into her hair and tapped it in a nervous rhythm on her desk.

"Oh, come, Robert. During the last month every time I looked at you your mind was a million miles away. Now,

41

what is it? Just making plans for vacation, or, perhaps, some trouble with the boys?"

"I'm not having trouble with anybody, Miss Gildea."

"You don't seem to understand, Robert, that I'm not trying to punish you for anything. Your homework is good. You've managed to keep up with the class, but I do think your inattentiveness should be explained. What, for example, were you thinking this afternoon when I spoke to you directly for five minutes, and you didn't hear a word I said?"

"Nothing, Miss Gildea."

She brought the pencil down sharply on the desk. "There must have been *something*, Robert. Now, I must insist that that you think back, and try to explain yourself."

Looking at his impassive face she knew that somehow she herself had been put on the defensive, that if any means of graceful retreat were offered now she would gladly take it. Thirty-eight years, she thought grimly, and I'm still trying to play mother hen to ducklings. Not that there wasn't a bright side to the picture. Thirty-eight years passed meant only two more to go before retirement, the half-salary pension, the chance to putter around the house, tend to the garden properly. The pension wouldn't buy you furs and diamonds, sure enough, but it could buy the right to enjoy your own home for the rest of your days instead of a dismal room in the County Home for Old Ladies. Miss Gildea had visited the County Home once, on an instructional visit, and preferred not to think about it.

"Well, Robert," she said wearily, "have you remembered what you were thinking?"

"Yes, Miss Gildea."

"What was it?"

"I'd rather not tell, Miss Gildea."

42

"I insist!"

"Well," Robert said gently, "I was thinking I wished you were dead, Miss Gildea. I was thinking I wished I could kill you."

Her first reaction was simply blank incomprehension. She had been standing not ten feet away when that car had skidded up on the sidewalk and crushed her mother's life from her, and Miss Gildea had neither screamed nor fainted. She had stood there dumbly, because of the very unreality of the thing. Just the way she stood in court where they explained that the man got a year in jail, but didn't have a dime to pay for the tragedy he had brought about. And now the orderly ranks of desks before her, the expanse of blackboard around her, and Robert's face in the midst of it all were no more real. She found herself rising from her chair, walking toward Robert, who shrank back, his eyes wide and panicky, his elbow half lifted as if to ward off a blow.

"Do you understand what you've just said?" Miss Gildea demanded hoarsely.

"No, Miss Gildea! Honest, I didn't mean anything."

She shook her head unbelievingly. "Whatever made you say it? Whatever in the world could make a boy say a thing like that, such a wicked, terrible thing!"

"You wanted to know! You kept asking me!"

The sight of that protective elbow raised against her cut as deep as the incredible words had.

"Put that arm down!" Miss Gildea said shrilly, and then struggled to get her voice under control. "In all my years I've never struck a child, and I don't intend to start now!"

Robert dropped his arm and clasped his hands together on his desk, and Miss Gildea, looking at the pinched white knuckles, realized with surprise that her own hands were shaking uncontrollably. "But if you think this little matter ends here, young-feller-me-lad," she said, "you've got another thought coming. You get your things together, and we're marching right up to Mr. Harkness. He'll be very much interested in all this."

Mr. Harkness was the Principal. He had arrived only the term before, and but for his taste in eyeglasses (the large, black-rimmed kind which, Miss Gildea privately thought, looked actorish) and his predilection for the phrase "modern pedagogical methods" was, in her opinion, a rather engaging young man.

He looked at Robert's frightened face and then at Miss Gildea's pursed lips. "Well," he said pleasantly, "what seems to be the trouble here?"

"That," said Miss Gildea, "is something I think Robert should tell you about."

She placed a hand on Robert's shoulder, but he pulled away and backed slowly toward Mr. Harkness, his breath coming in loud, shuddering sobs, his eyes riveted on Miss Gildea as if she were the only thing in the room beside himself. Mr. Harkness put an arm around Robert and frowned at Miss Gildea.

"Now, what's behind all this, Miss Gildea? The boy seems frightened to death."

Miss Gildea found herself sick of it all, anxious to get out of the room, away from Robert. "That's enough, Robert," she commanded. "Just tell Mr. Harkness exactly what happened."

"I said the boy was frightened to death, Miss Gildea," Mr. Harkness said brusquely. "We'll talk about it as soon as he understands we're his friends. Won't we, Robert?"

Robert shook his head vehemently. "I didn't do anything bad! Miss Gildea said I didn't do anything bad!"

"Well, then!" said Mr. Harkness triumphantly. "There's nothing to be afraid of, is there?"

Robert shook his head again. "She said I had to stay in after school."

Mr. Harkness glanced sharply at Miss Gildea. "I suppose he missed the morning bus, is that it? And after I said a directive that the staff was to make allowances—"

"Robert doesn't use a bus," Miss Gildea protested. "Perhaps I'd better explain all this, Mr. Harkness. You see—"

"I think Robert's doing very well," Mr. Harkness said, and tightened his arm around Robert, who nodded shakily.

"She kept me in," he said, "and then when we were alone she came up close to me and she said, 'I know what you're thinking. You're thinking you'd like to see me dead! You're thinking you'd like to kill me, aren't you?'"

Robert's voice had dropped to an eerie whisper that bound Miss Gildea like a spell. It was broken only when she saw the expression on Mr. Harkness's face.

"Why, that's a lie!" she cried. "That's the most dreadful lie I ever heard any boy dare—"

Mr. Harkness cut in abruptly. "Miss Gildea! I *insist* you let the boy finish what he has to say."

Miss Gildea's voice fluttered. "It seems to me, Mr. Harkness, that he has been allowed to say quite enough already!"

"Has he?" Mr. Harkness asked.

"Robert has been inattentive lately, especially so this afternoon. After class I asked him what he had been thinking about, and he dared to say he was thinking how he wished I were dead! How he wanted to kill me!"

"Robert said that?"

"In almost those exact words. And I can tell you, Mr.

Harkness, that I was shocked, terribly shocked, especially since Robert always seemed like such a nice boy."

"His record—?"

"His record is quite good. It's just—"

"And his social conduct?" asked Mr. Harkness in the same level voice.

"As far as I know, he gets along with the other children well enough."

"But for some reason," persisted Mr. Harkness, "you found him annoying you."

Robert raised his voice. "I didn't! Miss Gildea said I didn't do anything bad. And I always liked her. I like her better than *any* teacher!"

Miss Gildea fumbled blindly in her hair for the silver pencil, and failed to find it. She looked around the floor distractedly.

"Yes?" said Mr. Harkness.

"My pencil," said Miss Gildea on the verge of tears. "It's gone."

"Surely, Miss Gildea," said Mr. Harkness in a tone of mild exasperation, "this is not quite the moment—"

"It was very valuable," Miss Gildea tried to explain hopelessly. "It was my mother's." In the face of Mr. Harkness's stony surveillance she knew she must look a complete mess. Hems crooked, nose red, hair all disheveled. "I'm all upset, Mr. Harkness. It's been a long term and now all this right at the end of it. I don't know what to say."

Mr. Harkness's face fell into sympathetic lines.

"That's quite all right, Miss Gildea. I know how you feel. Now, if you want to leave, I think Robert and I should have a long, friendly talk."

"If you don't mind—"

46

"No, no," Mr. Harkness said heartily. "As a matter of fact, I think that would be the best thing all around."

After he had seen her out he closed the door abruptly behind her, and Miss Gildea walked heavily up the stairway and down the corridor to the Sixth Grade room: The silver pencil was there on the floor at Robert's desk, and she picked it up and carefully polished it with her handkerchief. Then she sat down at her desk with the handkerchief to her nose and wept soundlessly for ten minutes.

That night, when the bitter taste of humiliation had grown faint enough to permit it, Miss Gildea reviewed the episode with all the honesty at her command. Honesty with oneself had always been a major point in her credo, had, in fact, been passed on through succeeding classes during the required lesson on The Duties of an American Citizen, when Miss Gildea, to sum up the lesson, would recite: "This above all, To thine ownself be true . . ." while thumping her fist on her desk as an accompaniment to each syllable.

Hamlet, of course, was not in the syllabus of the Sixth Grade, whose reactions over the years never deviated from a mixed bewilderment and indifference. But Miss Gildea, after some prodding of the better minds into a discussion of the lines, would rest content with the knowledge that she had sown good seed on what, she prayed, was fertile ground.

Reviewing the case of Robert now, with her emotions under control, she came to the unhappy conclusion that it was she who had committed the injustice. The child had been ordered to stay after school, something that to him could mean only a punishment. He had been ordered to disclose some shadowy, childlike thoughts that had drifted through his mind hours before, and, unable to do so, either had to

47

make up something out of the whole cloth, or blurt out the immediate thought in his immature mind.

It was hardly unusual, reflected Miss Gildea sadly, for a child badgered by a teacher to think what Robert had; she could well remember her own feelings toward a certain pompadoured harridan who still haunted her dreams. And the only conclusion to be drawn, unpleasant though it was, was that Robert, and not she, had truly put into practice those beautiful words from Shakespeare.

It was this, as well as the sight of his pale accusing face before her while she led the class through the morning session next day, which prompted her to put Robert in charge of refilling the water pitcher during recess. The duties of the water pitcher monitor were to leave the playground a little before the rest of the class and clean and refill the pitcher on her desk, but since the task was regarded as an honor by the class, her gesture, Miss Gildea felt with some self-approval, carried exactly the right note of conciliation.

She was erasing the blackboard at the front of the room near the end of the recess when she heard Robert approaching her desk, but much as she wanted to she could not summon up courage enough to turn and face him. As if, she thought, he were the teacher, and I were afraid of him. And she could feel her cheeks grow warm at the thought.

He reentered the room on the sound of the bell that marked the end of recess, and this time Miss Gildea plopped the eraser firmly into its place beneath the blackboard and turned to look at him. "Thank you very much, Robert," she said as he set the pitcher down and neatly capped it with her drinking glass.

"You're welcome, Miss Gildea," Robert said politely. He drew a handkerchief from his pocket, wiped his hands with it, then smiled gently at Miss Gildea. "I bet you think I put poison or something into that water," he said gravely, "but I wouldn't do anything like that, Miss Gildea. Honest, I wouldn't."

Miss Gildea gasped, then reached out a hand toward Robert's shoulder. She withdrew it hastily when he shrank away with the familiar panicky look in his eyes.

"Why did you say that, Robert?" Miss Gildea demanded in a terrible voice. "That was plain impudence, wasn't it? You thought you were being smart, didn't you?"

At that moment the rest of the class surged noisily into the room, but Miss Gildea froze them into silence with a commanding wave of the hand. Out of the corner of her eye she noted the cluster of shocked and righteous faces allied with her in condemnation, and she felt a quick little sense of triumph in her position.

"I was talking to you, Robert," she said. "What do you have to say for yourself?"

Robert took another step backward and almost tumbled over a schoolbag left carelessly in the aisle. He caught himself, then stood there helplessly, his eyes never leaving Miss Gildea's.

"Well, Robert?"

He shook his head wildly. "I didn't do it!" he cried. "I didn't put anything in your water, Miss Gildea! I told you I didn't!"

Without looking, Miss Gildea knew that the cluster of accusing faces had swung toward her now, felt her triumph turn to a sick bewilderment inside her. It was as if Robert, with his teary eyes and pale, frightened face and too-large ears, had turned into a strange jellylike creature that could not be pinned down and put in its place. As if he were retreating further and further down some dark, twisting path, and leading her on with him. And, she thought desperately, she had to pull herself free before she did something dreadful, something unforgivable.

She couldn't take the boy to Mr. Harkness again. Not only did the memory of that scene in his office the day before make her shudder, but a repeated visit would be an admission that after thirty-eight years of teaching she was not up to the mark of a disciplinarian.

But for her sake, if for nothing else, Robert had to be put in his place. With a gesture, Miss Gildea ordered the rest of the class to their seats and turned to Robert, who remained standing.

"Robert," said Miss Gildea, "I want an apology for what has just happened."

"I'm sorry, Miss Gildea," Robert said, and it looked as if his eyes would be brimming with tears in another moment.

Miss Gildea hardened her heart to this. *"I apologize, Miss Gildea, and it will not happen again,"* she prompted.

Miraculously, Robert contained his tears. "I apologize, Miss Gildea, and it will not happen again," he muttered and dropped limply into his seat.

"Well!" said Miss Gildea, drawing a deep breath as she looked around at the hushed class. "Perhaps that will be a lesson to us all."

The classroom work did not go well after that, but, as Miss Gildea told herself, there were only a few days left to the end of the term, and after that, praise be, there was the garden, the comfortable front porch of the old house to share with neighbors in the summer evenings, and then next term a new set of faces in the classroom, with Robert's not among them.

Later, closing the windows of the room after the class had left, Miss Gildea was brought up short by the sight of a large group gathered on the sidewalk near the parked buses. It was Robert, she saw, surrounded by most of the Sixth Grade, and obviously the center of interest. He was nodding emphatically when she put her face to the window, and she drew back quickly at the sight, moved by some queer sense of guilt.

Only a child, she assured herself, *he's only a child*, but that thought did not in any way dissolve the anger against him that struck like a lump in her throat.

That was on Thursday. By Tuesday of the next week, the final week of the term, Miss Gildea was acutely conscious of the oppressive atmosphere lying over the classroom. Ordinarily, the awareness of impending vacation acted on the class like a violent agent dropped into some inert liquid. There would be ferment and seething beneath the surface, manifested by uncontrollable giggling and whispering, and this would grow more and more turbulent until all restraint and discipline was swept away in the general upheaval of excitement and good spirits.

That, Miss Gildea thought, was the way it always had been, but it was strangely different now. The Sixth Grade, down to the most irrepressible spirits in it, acted as if it had been turned to a set of robots before her startled eyes. Hands tightly clasped on desks, eyes turned toward her with an almost frightening intensity, the class responded to her mildest requests as if they were shouted commands. And when she walked down the aisles between them, one and all seemed to have adopted Robert's manner of shrinking away fearfully at her approach.

Miss Gildea did not like to think of what all this might mean, but valiantly forced herself to do so. Can it mean, she asked herself, that all think as Robert does, are choosing

51

this way of showing it? And, if they knew how cruel it was, would they do it?

Other teachers, Miss Gildea knew, sometimes took problems such as this to the Teachers' Room where they could be studied and answered by those who saw them in an objective light. It might be that the curious state of the Sixth Grade was being duplicated in other classes. Perhaps she herself was imagining the whole thing, or, frightening thought, looking back, as people will when they grow old, on the sort of past that never really did exist. Why, in that case—and Miss Gildea had to laugh at herself with a faint merriment—she would just find herself reminiscing about her thirty-eight years of teaching to some bored young woman who didn't have the fraction of experience she did.

But underneath the current of these thoughts, Miss Gildea knew there was one honest reason for not going to the Teachers' Room this last week of the term. She had received no gifts, not one. And the spoils from each grade heaped high in a series of pyramids against the wall, the boxes of fractured cookies, the clumsily wrapped jars of preserves, the scarves, the stockings, the handkerchiefs, infinite, endless boxes of handkerchiefs, all were there to mark the triumph of each teacher. And Miss Gildea, who in all her years at District School Number Three had been blushingly proud of the way her pyramid was highest at the end of each term, had not yet received a single gift from the Sixth Grade class.

After the class was dismissed that afternoon, however, the spell was broken. Only a few of her pupils still loitered in the hallway near the door, Miss Gildea noted, but Robert remained in his seat. Then, as she gathered together her belongings, Robert approached her with a box outheld in his hand. It was, from its shape, a box of candy, and, as Miss

Gildea could tell from the wrapping, expensive candy. Automatically, she reached a hand out, then stopped herself short. He'll never make up to me for what he's done, she told herself furiously; I'll never let him.

"Yes, Robert?" she said coolly.

"It's a present for you, Miss Gildea," Robert said, and then as Miss Gildea watched in fascination he began to strip the wrappings from it. He laid the paper neatly on the desk and lifted the cover of the box to display the chocolates within. "My mother said that's the biggest box they had," he said wistfully. "Don't you even want them, Miss Gildea?"

Miss Gildea weakened despite herself. "Did you think I would, after what's happened, Robert?" she asked.

Robert reflected a moment. "Well," he said at last, "if you want me to, I'll eat one right in front of you, Miss Gildea."

Miss Gildea recoiled as if at a faraway warning. *Don't let him say any more,* something inside her cried; *he's only playing a trick, another horrible trick,* and then she was saying, "Why would I want you to do that, Robert?"

"So you'll see they're not poison or anything, Miss Gildea," Robert said. "Then you'll believe it, won't you, Miss Gildea?"

She had been prepared. Even before he said the words, she had felt her body drawing itself tighter and tighter against what she knew was coming. But the sound of the words themselves only served to release her like a spring coiled too tightly.

"You little monster!" sobbed Miss Gildea and struck wildly at the proferred box, which flew almost to the far wall, while chocolates cascaded stickily around the room. "How dare you!" she cried. "How dare you!" and her small bony fists beat at Robert's cowering shoulders and back as he tried to retreat.

He half turned in the aisle, slipped on a piece of chocolate, and went down to his knees, but before he could recover himself Miss Gildea was on him again, her lips drawn back, her fists pummeling him as if they were a pair of tireless mallets. Robert had started to scream at the top of his lungs from the first blow, but it was no more than a remote buzzing in Miss Gildea's ears.

"Miss Gildea!"

That was Mr. Harkness's voice, she knew, and those must be Mr. Harkness's hands which pulled her away so roughly that she had to keep herself from falling by clutching at her desk. She stood there weakly, feeling the wild fluttering of her heart, feeling the sick churning of shame and anguish in her while she tried to bring the room into focus again. There was the knot of small excited faces peering through the open doorway, they must have called Mr. Harkness, and Mr. Harkness himself listening to Robert who talked and wept alternately, and there was a mess everywhere. Of course, thought Miss Gildea dazedly, those must be chocolate stains. Chocolate stains all over my lovely clean room.

Then Robert was gone, the faces at the door were gone, and the door itself was closed behind them. Only Mr. Harkness remained, and Miss Gildea watched him as he removed his glasses, cleaned them carefully, and then held them up at arm's length and studied them before settling them once more on his nose.

"Well, Miss Gildea," said Mr. Harkness as if he were speaking to the glasses rather than to her, "this is a serious business."

Miss Gildea nodded.

"I am sick," Mr. Harkness said quietly, "really sick at the thought that somewhere in this school, where I tried to

54

introduce decent pedagogical standards, corporal punishment is still being practiced."

"That's not fair at all, Mr. Harkness," Miss Gildea said shakily. "I hit the boy, that's true, and I know I was wrong to do it, but that is the first time in all my life I raised a finger against any child. And if you knew my feelings—"

"Ah," said Mr. Harkness, "that's exactly what I would like to know, Miss Gildea." He nodded to her chair, and she sat down weakly. "Now, just go ahead and explain everything as you saw it."

It was a difficult task, made even more difficult by the fact that Mr. Harkness chose to stand facing the window. Forced to address his back this way, Miss Gildea found that she had the sensation of speaking in a vacuum, but she mustered the facts as well as she could, presented them with strong emotion, and then sank back in the chair quite exhausted.

Mr. Harkness remained silent for a long while, then slowly turned to face Miss Gildea. "I am not a practicing psychiatrist," he said at last, "although as an educator I have, of course, taken a considerable interest in that field. But I do not think it needs a practitioner to tell what a clear-cut and obvious case I am facing here. Nor," he added sympathetically, "what a tragic one."

"It might simply be," suggested Miss Gildea, "that Robert—"

"I am not speaking about Robert," said Mr. Harkness soberly, quietly.

It took an instant for this to penetrate, and then Miss Gildea felt the blood cold in her.

"Do you think I'm lying about all this?" she cried incredulously. "Can you possibly—"

"I am sure," Mr. Harkness replied soothingly, "that you

were describing things exactly as you saw them, Miss Gildea. But—have you ever heard the phrase 'persecution complex'? Do you think you could recognize the symptoms of that condition if they were presented objectively? I can, Miss Gildea. I assure you, I can."

Miss Gildea struggled to speak, but the words seemed to choke her. "No," she managed to say, "you couldn't! Because some mischievous boy chooses to make trouble—"

"Miss Gildea, no child of eleven, however mischievous, could draw the experiences Robert has described to me out of his imagination. He has discussed these experiences with me at length; now I have heard your side of the case. And the conclusions to be drawn, I must say, are practically forced on me."

The room started to slip out of focus again, and Miss Gildea frantically tried to hold it steady.

"But that just means you're taking his word against mine!" she said fiercely.

"Unfortunately, Miss Gildea, not his word alone. Last weekend, a delegation of parents met the School Board and made it quite plain that they were worried because of what their children told them of your recent actions. A dozen children in your class described graphically at that meeting how you had accused them of trying to poison your drinking water, and how you had threatened them because of this. And Robert, it may interest you to know, was not even one of them.

"The School Board voted your dismissal then and there, Miss Gildea, but in view of your long years of service it was left for me to override that decision if I wished to on my sole responsibility. After this episode, however, I cannot see that I have any choice. I must do what is best."

"Dismissal?" said Miss Gildea vaguely. "But they can't. I

only have two more years to go. They can't do that, Mr. Harkness; all they're trying to do is trick me out of my pension!"

"Believe me," said Mr. Harkness gently, "they're not trying to do anything of the sort, Miss Gildea. Nobody in the world is trying to hurt you. I give you my solemn word that the only thing which has entered into consideration of this case from first to last has been the welfare of the children."

The room swam in sunlight, but under it Miss Gildea's face was gray and lifeless. She reached forward to fill her glass with water, stopped short, and seemed to gather herself together with a sudden brittle determination. "I'll just have to speak to the Board myself," she said in a high breathless voice. "That's the only thing to do, go there and explain the whole thing to them!"

"That would not help," said Mr. Harkness pityingly. "Believe, Miss Gildea, it would not."

Miss Gildea left her chair and came to him, her eyes wide and frightened. She laid a trembling hand on his arm and spoke eagerly, quickly, trying to make him understand. "You see," she said, "that means I won't get my pension. I must have two more years for that, don't you see? There's the payment on the house, the garden—no, the garden is part of the house, really—but without the pension—"

She was pulling furiously at his arm with every phrase as if she could drag him bodily into a comprehension of her words, but he stood unyielding and only shook his head pityingly. "You must control yourself, Miss Gildea," he pleaded. "You're not yourself, and it's impossible—"

"No!" she cried in a strange voice. "No!"

When she pulled away he knew almost simultaneously what she intended to do, but the thought froze him to the spot, and when he moved it was too late. He burst into the

57

corridor through the door she had flung open, and almost threw himself down the stairway to the main hall. The door to the street was just swinging shut and he ran toward it, one hand holding the rim of his glasses, a sharp little pain digging into his side, but before he could reach the door he heard the screech of brakes, the single agonized scream, and the horrified shout of a hundred shrill voices.

He put his hand on the door, but could not find the strength to open it. A few minutes later, a cleaning woman had to sidle around him to get outside and see what all the excitement was about.

Miss Reardon, the substitute, took the Sixth Grade the next day, and, everything considered, handled it very well. The single ripple in the even current of the session came at its very start when Miss Reardon explained her presence by referring to the "sad accident that happened to dear Miss Gildea." The mild hubbub which followed this contained several voices, notably in the back of the room, which protested plaintively, "It was *not* an accident, Miss Reardon; she ran right in front of that bus," but Miss Reardon quickly brought order to the room with a few sharp raps of her ruler, and after that, classwork was carried on in a pleasant and orderly fashion.

Robert walked home slowly that afternoon, swinging his schoolbag placidly at his side, savoring the June warmth soaking into him, the fresh green smell in the air, the memory of Miss Reardon's understanding face so often turned toward his in eager and friendly interest. His home was identical with all the others on the block, square white boxes with small lawns before them, and its only distinction was that all its blinds were drawn down. After he had closed the front door very quietly behind him, he set his schoolbag down in the hallway, and went into the stuffy half-darkness of the living room.

Robert's father sat in the big armchair in his bathrobe, the way he always did, and Robert's mother was bent over him holding a glass of water.

"No!" Robert's father said. "You just want to get rid of me, but I won't let you! I know what you put into it, and I won't drink it! I'll die before I drink it!"

"Please," Robert's mother said, "please take it. I swear it's only water. I'll drink some myself if you don't believe me." But when she drank a little and then held the glass to his lips, Robert's father only tossed his head from side to side.

Robert stood there watching the scene with fascination, his lips moving in silent mimicry of the familiar words. Then he cleared his throat.

"I'm home, Mama," Robert said softly. "Can I have some milk and cookies, please?"

F. MARION CRAWFORD

The Doll's Ghost

It was a terrible accident, and for one moment the splendid machinery of Cranston House got out of gear and stood still. The butler emerged from the retirement in which he spent his elegant leisure, two grooms appeared simultaneously, there were actually housemaids on the grand staircase, and Mrs. Pringle herself stood upon the landing. Mrs. Pringle was the housekeeper. As for the head nurse, the under nurse, and the nursery maid, their feelings cannot be described.

The Lady Gwendolen Lancaster-Douglas-Scroop, youngest daughter of the ninth Duke of Cranston, and aged six years and three months, picked herself up quite alone, and sat down on the third step from the foot of the grand staircase in Cranston House.

"Oh!" ejaculated the butler, and he disappeared again.

"Ah!" responded the grooms as they also went away.

"It's only that doll," Mrs. Pringle was distinctly heard to say, in a tone of contempt. Then the three nurses gathered round Lady Gwendolen and hurried her out of Cranston House as fast as they could, lest it should be found out upstairs that they had allowed the Lady Gwendolen to tumble down the grand staircase with her doll in her arms. And as the doll was badly broken, the nursery maid carried it, with the pieces, wrapped up in Lady Gwendolen's little cloak. It was not far to Hyde Park, and when they had reached a quiet place they took means to find out that Lady Gwendolen had no bruises.

Lady Gwendolen Lancaster-Douglas-Scroop sometimes yelled, but she never cried. It was because she had yelled that the nurse had allowed her to go downstairs alone with Nina, the doll, under one arm, while she steadied herself with her other hand on the balustrade, and trod upon the polished marble steps beyond the edge of the carpet. So she had fallen, and Nina had come to grief.

When the nurses were quite sure that she was not hurt, they unwrapped the doll and looked at her in her turn. She had been a very beautiful doll, very large, and fair, and healthy, with real yellow hair, and eyelids that would open and shut over very grown-up dark eyes. Moreover, when you moved her right arm up and down she said "Pa-pa," and when you moved the left she said "Ma-ma," very distinctly.

"I heard her say 'Pa' when she fell," said the under nurse, who heard everything. "But she ought to have said 'Pa-pa.'"

"That's because her arm went up when she hit the step," said the head nurse. "She'll say the other 'Pa' when I put it down again."

"Pa," said Nina, as her right arm was pushed down, and speaking through her broken face. It was cracked right across, from the upper corner of the forehead, with a hideous gash, through the nose and down to the little frilled collar of the pale green silk Mother Hubbard frock, and two little three-cornered pieces of porcelain had fallen out.

"It's a wonder she can speak at all, being all smashed," said the under nurse.

"You'll have to take her to Mr. Puckler," said her superior. "It's not far, and you'd better go at once." The under nurse wrapped Nina up again and departed.

Mr. Bernard Puckler and his little daughter lived in a little house in a little alley, which led out off a quiet little street not very far from Belgrave Square. He was the great doll doctor, and his extensive practice lay in the most aristocratic quarter. He mended dolls of all sizes and ages, boy dolls and girl dolls, baby dolls in long clothes, and grown-up dolls in fashionable gowns, talking dolls and dumb dolls, those that shut their eyes when they lay down, and those whose eyes had to be shut for them by means of a mysterious wire. His daughter, Else, was only just over twelve years old, but she was already very clever at mending dolls' clothes, and at doing their hair, which is harder than you might think, though the dolls sit quite still while it is being done.

Mr. Puckler had originally been a German, but he had dissolved his nationality in the ocean of London many years ago, like a great many foreigners. He still had one or two German friends, however, who came on Saturday evenings, and smoked with him and played piquet or "skat" with him for farthing points, and called him "Herr Doctor," which seemed to please Mr. Puckler very much.

He looked older than he was, for his beard was rather long and ragged, his hair was grizzled and thin, and he wore horn-rimmed spectacles. As for Else, she was a thin, pale child, very quiet and neat, with dark eyes and brown hair that was plaited down her back and tied with a bit of black ribbon. She mended the dolls' clothes and took the dolls back to their homes when they were quite strong again.

The house was a little one, but too big for the two people who lived in it. There was a small sitting room on the street, and the workshop was at the back, and there were three rooms upstairs. But the father and daughter lived most of their time in the workshop, because they were generally at work, even in the evenings.

Mr. Puckler laid Nina on the table and looked at her a long time, till the tears began to fill his eyes behind the horn-rimmed spectacles. He was a very susceptible man, and he often fell in love with the dolls he mended, and found it hard to part with them when they had smiled at him for a few days. They were real little people to him, with characters and thoughts and feelings of their own, and he was very tender with them all. But some attracted him especially from the first, and when they were brought to him maimed and injured, their state seemed so pitiful to him that the tears came easily. You must remember that he had lived among dolls during a great part of his life, and understood them.

"How do you know that they feel nothing?" he went on to say to Else. "You must be gentle with them. It costs nothing to be kind to the little beings, and perhaps it makes a difference to them."

And Else understood him, because she was a child, and she knew that she was more to him than all the dolls.

He fell in love with Nina at first sight, perhaps because her beautiful brown glass eyes were something like Else's own, and he loved Else first and best, with all his heart. And, besides, it was a very sorrowful case. Nina had evidently not been long in the world, for her complexion was perfect, her hair was smooth where it should be smooth, and curly where it should be curly, and her silk clothes were perfectly new. But across her face was that frightful gash, like a saber cut, deep and shadowy within, but clean and sharp at the edges. When he tenderly pressed her head to close the gaping wound, the edges made a fine grating sound, that was painful to hear, and the lids of the dark eyes quivered and trembled as though Nina were suffering dreadfully.

"Poor Nina!" he exclaimed sorrowfully. "But I shall not hurt you much, though you will take a long time to get strong."

He always asked the names of the broken dolls when they were brought to him, and sometimes the people knew what the children called them, and told him. He liked "Nina" for a name. Altogether and in every way she pleased him more than any doll he had seen for many years, and he felt drawn to her, and made up his mind to make her perfectly strong and sound, no matter how much labor it cost him.

Mr. Puckler worked patiently and Else watched him. She could do nothing for poor Nina, whose clothes needed no mending. The longer the doll doctor worked, the more fond he became of the yellow hair and the beautiful brown glass eyes. He sometimes forgot all the other dolls that were waiting to be mended, lying side by side on a shelf, and sat for an hour gazing at Nina's face, while he racked his ingenuity for some new invention by which to hide even the smallest trace of the terrible accident.

She was wonderfully mended. Even he was obliged to admit that; but the scar was still visible to his keen eyes, a very fine line right across the face, downward from right to left. Yet all the conditions had been most favorable for a cure, since the cement had set quite hard at the first attempt and the weather had been fine and dry, which makes a great difference in a dolls' hospital.

At last he knew that he could do no more, and the under nurse had already come twice to see whether the job was finished, as she coarsely expressed it.

"Nina is not quite strong yet," Mr. Puckler had answered each time, for he could not make up his mind to face the parting.

And now he sat before the square deal table at which he worked, and Nina lay before him for the last time with a big brown paper box beside her. It stood there like her coffin, waiting for her, he thought. He must put her into it, and lay tissue paper over her dear face, and then put on the lid, and at the thought of tying the string his sight was dim with tears again. He was never to look into the glassy depths of the beautiful brown eyes any more, nor to hear the little wooden voice say "Pa-pa" and "Ma-ma." It was a very painful moment.

In the vain hope of gaining time before the separation, he took up the little sticky bottles of cement and glue and gum and color, looking at each one in turn, and then at Nina's face. And all his small tools lay there, neatly arranged in a row, but he knew that he could not use them again for Nina. She was quite strong at last, and in a country where there should be no cruel children to hurt her she might live a hundred years, with only that almost imperceptible line across her face to tell of the fearful thing that had befallen her on the marble steps of Cranston House.

Suddenly Mr. Puckler's heart was quite full, and he rose abruptly from his seat and turned away.

"Else," he said unsteadily, "you must do it for me. I cannot bear to see her go into the box."

So he went and stood at the window with his back turned, while Else did what he had not the heart to do.

"Is it done?" he asked, not turning round. "Then take her away, my dear. Put on your hat, and take her to Cranston House quickly, and when you are gone I will turn round."

Else was used to her father's queer ways with the dolls, and though she had never seen him so much moved by a parting, she was not much surprised.

"Come back quickly," he said, when he heard her hand on the latch. "It is growing late, and I should not send you at this hour. But I cannot bear to look forward to it any more."

When Else was gone, he left the window and sat down in his place before the table again, to wait for the child to come back. He touched the place where Nina had lain, very gently, and he realled the softly tinted pink face, and the glass eyes, and the ringlets of yellow hair, till he could almost see them.

The evenings were long, for it was late in the spring. But it began to grow dark soon, and Mr. Puckler wondered why Else did not come back. She had been gone an hour and a half, and that was much longer than he had expected, for it was barely half a mile from Belgrave Square to Cranston House. He reflected that the child might have been kept waiting, but as the twilight deepened he grew anxious, and walked up and down in the grim workshop, no longer thinking of Nina, but of Else, his own living child, whom he loved.

An undefinable, disquieting sensation came upon him by fine degrees, a chilliness and a faint stirring of his thin hair, joined with a wish to be in any company rather than to be alone much longer. It was the beginning of fear.

He told himself in strong German-English that he was a

foolish old man, and he began to feel about for the matches in the dusk. He knew just where they should be, for he always kept them in the same place, close to the little tin box that held bits of sealing wax of various colors, for some kinds of mending. But somehow he could not find the matches in the gloom.

Something had happened to Else, he was sure, and as his fear increased, he felt as though it might be allayed if he could get a light and see what time it was. Then he called himself a foolish old man again, and the sound of his own voice startled him in the dark. He could not find the matches.

The window was gray still; he might see what time it was if he went close to it, and he could go and get matches out of the cupboard afterwards. He stood back from the table, to get out of the way of the chair, and began to cross the board floor.

Something was following him in the dark. There was a small pattering, as of tiny feet upon the boards. He stopped and listened, and the roots of his hair tingled. It was nothing, and he was a foolish old man. He made two steps more, and he was sure that he heard the little pattering again. He turned his back to the window, leaning against the sash so that the panes began to crack, and he faced the dark. Everything was quite still, and it smelt of paste and cement and wood filings as usual.

"Is that you, Else?" he asked, and he was surprised by the fear in his voice.

There was no answer in the room, and he held up his watch and tried to make out what time it was by the gray dusk that was just not darkness. So far as he could see, it was within two or three minutes of ten o'clock. He had been a long time alone. He was shocked, and frightened for Else, out in London, so late, and he almost ran across the room to the door. As he fumbled for the latch, he distinctly heard the running of the little feet after him.

"Mice!" he exclaimed feebly, just as he got the door open.

He shut it quickly behind him, and felt as though some cold thing had settled on his back and were writhing upon him. The passage was quite dark, but he found his hat and was out in the alley in a moment, breathing more freely, and surprised to find how much light there still was in the open air. He could see the pavement clearly under his feet, and far off in the street to which the alley led he could hear the laughter and calls of children, playing some game out of doors. He wondered how he could have been so nervous, and for an instant he thought of going back into the house to wait quietly for Else. But instantly he felt that nervous fright of something stealing over him again. In any case it was better to walk up to Cranston House and ask the servants about the child. One of the women had perhaps taken a fancy to her, and was even now giving her tea and cake.

He walked quickly to Belgrave Square, and then up the broad streets, listening as he went, whenever there was no other sound, for the tiny footsteps. But he heard nothing, and was laughing at himself when he rang the servants' bell at the big house. Of course, the child must be there.

The person who opened the door was quite an inferior person, for it was a back door, but affected the manners of the front, and stared at Mr. Puckler superciliously under the strong light.

No little girl had been seen, and he knew "nothing about no dolls."

"She is my little girl," said Mr. Puckler tremulously, for all his anxiety was returning tenfold, "and I am afraid something has happened."

The inferior person said rudely that "nothing could have happened to her in that house, because she had not been there, which was a jolly good reason why"; and Mr. Puckler was obliged to admit that the man ought to know, as it was his business to keep the door and let people in. He wished to be allowed to speak to the under nurse, who knew him; but the man was ruder than ever, and finally shut the door in his face.

When the doll doctor was alone in the street, he steadied himself by the railing, for he felt as though he were breaking in two, just as some dolls break, in the middle of the backbone.

Presently he knew that he must be doing something to find Else, and that gave him strength. He began to walk as quickly as he could through the streets, following every highway and byway which his little girl might have taken on her errand. He also asked several policemen in vain if they had seen her, and most of them answered him kindly, for they saw that he was a sober man and in his right senses, and some of them had little girls of their own.

It was one o'clock in the morning when he went up to his own door again, worn out and hopeless and brokenhearted. As he turned the key in the lock, his heart stood still, for he knew that he was awake and not dreaming, and that he really heard those tiny footsteps pattering to meet him inside the house.

But he was too unhappy to be much frightened any more, and his heart went on again with a dull regular pain, that found its way all through him with every pulse. So he went in, and hung up his hat in the dark, and found the matches in the cupboard and the candlestick in its place in the corner.

Mr. Puckler was so much overcome and so completely

worn out that he sat down in his chair before the worktable and almost fainted, as his face dropped forward upon his folded hands. Beside him the solitary candle burned steadily with a low flame in the still warm air.

"Else! Else!" he moaned against his yellow knuckles. And that was all he could say, and it was no relief to him. On the contrary, the very sound of the name was a new and sharp pain that pierced his ears and his head and his very soul. For every time he repeated the name it meant that little Else was dead, somewhere out in the streets of London in the dark.

He was so terribly hurt that he did not even feel something pulling gently at the skirt of his old coat, so gently that it was like the nibbling of a tiny mouse. He might have thought that it was really a mouse if he had noticed it.

"Else! Else!" he groaned right against his hands.

Then a cool breath stirred his thin hair, and the low flame of the one candle dropped down almost to a mere spark, not flickering as though a draft were going to blow it out, but just dropping down as if it were tired out. Mr. Puckler felt his hands stiffening with fright under his face; and there was a faint rustling sound, like some small silk thing blown in a gentle breeze. He sat up straight, stark and scared, and a small wooden voice spoke in the stillness.

"Pa-pa," it said, with a break between the syllables.

Mr. Puckler stood up in a single jump, and his chair fell over backward with a smashing noise upon the wooden floor. The candle had almost gone out.

It was Nina's doll voice, and he should have known it among the voices of a hundred other dolls. And yet there was something more in it, a little human ring, with a pitiful cry and a call for help, and the wail of a hurt child. Mr. Puckler stood up, stark and stiff, and tried to look round, but at first he could not, for he seemed to be frozen from head to foot.

Then he made a great effort, and he raised one hand to each of his temples, and pressed his own head round as he would have turned a doll's. The candle was burning so low that it might as well have been out altogether, for any light it gave, and the room seemed quite dark at first. Then he saw something. He would not have believed that he could be more frightened than he had been just before that. But he was, and his knees shook, for he saw the doll standing in the middle of the floor, shining with a faint and ghostly radiance, her beautiful glassy brown eyes fixed on his. And across her face the very thin line of the break he had mended with such care shone as though it were drawn in light with a fine point of white flame.

Yet there was something human, like Else's own, but as if only the doll saw him through them, and not Else. And there was enough of Else to bring back all his pain and to make him forget his fear.

"Else! My little Else!" he cried aloud.

The small ghost moved, and its doll-arm slowly rose and fell with a stiff, mechanical motion.

"Pa-pa," it said.

It seemed this time that there was even more of Else's tone echoing somewhere between the wooden notes that reached his ears so distinctly, and yet so far away. Else was calling him, he was sure.

His face was perfectly white in the gloom, but his knees did not shake anymore, and he felt that he was less frightened.

71

"Yes, child! But where? Where?" he asked. "Where are you, Else?"

"Pa-pa!"

The syllables died away in the quiet room. There was a low rustling of silk, the glassy brown eyes turned slowly away, and Mr. Puckler heard the pitter-patter of the small feet in the bronze kid slippers as the figure ran straight to the door. Then the candle burned high again, the room was full of light, and he was alone.

Mr. Puckler passed his hand over his eyes and looked about him. He could see everything quite clearly, and he felt that he must have been dreaming, though he was standing instead of sitting down, as he should have been if he had just waked up. The candle burned brightly now. There were the dolls to be mended, lying in a row with their toes up. The third one had lost her right shoe, and Else was making one. He knew that, and he was certainly not dreaming now. He had not been dreaming when he had come in from his fruitless search and had heard the doll's footsteps running to the door. He had not fallen asleep in his chair. How could he possibly have fallen asleep when his heart was breaking? He had been awake all the time.

He steadied himself, set the fallen chair upon its legs, and said to himself again very emphatically that he was a foolish old man. He ought to be out in the streets looking for his child, asking questions, and inquiring at the police stations, where all accidents were reported as soon as they were known, or at the hospitals.

"Pa-pa!"

The longing, wailing, pitiful little wooden cry rang from the passage, outside the door, and Mr. Puckler stood for an instant with white face, transfixed and rooted to the spot. A moment later his hand was on the latch. Then he was in the

passage, with the light streaming from the open door behind him.

Quite at the other end he saw the little phantom shining
clearly in the shadow, and the right hand seemed to beckon
to him as the arm rose and fell once more. He knew all at
once that it had not come to frighten him but to lead him,
and when it disappeared, and he walked boldly toward the
door, he knew that it was in the street outside, waiting for
him. He forgot that he was tired and had eaten no supper,
and had walked many miles, for a sudden hope ran through
and through him, like a golden stream of life.

And sure enough, at the corner of the alley, and at the
corner of the street, and out in Belgrave Square, he saw the
small ghost flitting before him. Sometimes it was only a
shadow, where there was other light, but then the glare of
the lamps made a pale green sheen on its little Mother Hubbard frock of silk; and sometimes, where the streets were
dark and silent, the whole figure shone out brightly, with its
yellow curls and rosy neck. It seemed to trot along like a
tiny child, and Mr. Puckler could almost hear the pattering
of the bronze kid slippers on the pavement as it ran. But it
went very fast, and he could only just keep up with it, tear-
ing along with his hat on the back of his head and his thin
hair blown by the night breeze, and his horn-rimmed spectacles firmly set upon his broad nose.

On and on he went, and he had no idea where he was. He
did not even care, for he knew certainly that he was going
the right way.

Then at last, in a wide, quiet street, he was standing
before a big, sober-looking door that had two lamps on
each side of it, and a polished brass bell-handle, which he
pulled.

And just inside, when the door was opened, in the bright

light, there was the little shadow, and the pale green sheen of the little silk dress, and once more the small cry came to his ears, less pitiful, more longing.

"Pa-pa!"

The shadow turned suddenly bright, and out of the brightness the beautiful brown glass eyes were turned up happily to his, while the rosy mouth smiled so divinely that the phantom doll looked almost like a little angel just then.

"A little girl was brought in soon after ten o'clock," said the quiet voice of the hospital doorkeeper. "I think they thought she was only stunned. She was holding a big brown paper box against her, and they could not get it out of her arms. She had a long plait of brown hair that hung down as they carried her."

"She is my little girl," said Mr. Puckler, but he hardly heard his own voice.

He leaned over Else's face in the gentle light of the children's ward, and when he had stood there a minute the beautiful brown eyes opened and looked up to his.

"Pa-pa!" cried Else, "I knew you would come!"

Then Mr. Puckler did not know what he did or said for a moment, and what he felt was worth all the fear and terror and despair that had almost killed him that night. But by and by Else was telling her story, and the nurse let her speak, for there were only two other children in the room, who were getting well and were sound asleep.

"They were big boys with bad faces," said Else, "and they tried to get Nina away from me, but I held on and fought as well as I could till one of them hit me with something, and I don't remember any more, for I tumbled down, and I suppose the boys ran away, and somebody found me there. But I'm afraid Nina is all smashed."

"Here is the box," said the nurse. "We could not take it out of her arms till she came to herself. Should you like to see if the doll is broken?"

And she undid the string cleverly, but Nina was all smashed to pieces. Only the gentle light of the children's ward made a pale green sheen in the folds of the little Mother Hubbard frock.

MARY NORTON

Paul's Tale

" 'Ho! Ho!' said the king, slapping his fat thighs. 'Methinks this youth shows promise.' But, at that moment, the court magician stepped forward . . . What *is* the matter, Paul? Don't you like this story?"

"Yes, I like it."

"Then lie quiet, dear, and listen."

"It was just a sort of stalk of a feather pushing itself through the eiderdown."

"Well, you needn't help it, dear. It's destructive. Where were we?" Aunt Isobel's nearsighted eyes searched down the page of the book. She looked comfortable and pink and plump, rocking there in the firelight. ". . . stepped forward . . . you see the court magician knew that the witch had taken the magic music box, and that Colin—Paul, you aren't listening!"

"Yes, I am. I can hear."

"Of course you can't hear—right under the bedclothes! What are you doing, dear?"

"I'm seeing what a hot water bottle feels like."

"Don't you know what a hot water bottle feels like?"

"I know what it feels like to me. I don't know what it feels like to itself."

"Well, shall I go on or not?"

"Yes, go on," said Paul. He emerged from the bedclothes, his hair ruffled.

Aunt Isobel looked at him curiously. He was her godson; he had a bad feverish cold; and his mother had gone to London. "Does it tire you, dear, to be read to?" she said at last.

"No. But I like told stories better than read stories."

Aunt Isobel got up and put some more coal on the fire. Then she looked at the clock. She sighed. "Well, dear," she said brightly, as she sat down once more on the rocking chair, "What sort of story would you like?" She unfolded her knitting.

"I'd like a real story."

"How do you mean, dear?" Aunt Isobel began to cast on. The cord of her pince-nez, anchored to her bosom, rose and fell in gentle undulations.

Paul flung around on his back, staring at the ceiling. *"You* know," he said, "quite real—so you know how it must have happened."

"Shall I tell you about Grace Darling?"

"No. Tell me about a little man."

"What sort of a little man?"

"A little man just as high—" Paul's eyes searched the room—"as that candlestick on the mantelshelf, but without the candle."

"But that's a very small candlestick. It's only about six inches."

"Well, about that big."

Aunt Isobel began knitting a few stitches. She was disappointed about the fairy story. She had been reading with so much expression, making a deep voice for the king, and a wicked, oily voice for the court magician, and a fine, cheerful, boyish voice for Colin, the swineherd. A little man—what could she say about a little man? "Ah," she exclaimed suddenly, and laid down her knitting, smiling at Paul. "Little men . . . of course . . ."

"Well," said Aunt Isobel, drawing in her breath. "Once upon a time, there was a little, tiny man, and he was no bigger than that candlestick—there on the mantelshelf."

Paul settled down, his cheek on his crook'd arm, his eyes on Aunt Isobel's face. The firelight flickered softly on the walls and ceiling.

"He was the sweetest little man you ever saw, and he wore a little red jerkin and a dear little cap made out of a foxglove. His boots . . ."

"He didn't have any," said Paul.

Aunt Isobel looked startled. "Yes," she exclaimed. "He had boots—little, pointed—"

"He didn't have any clothes," contradicted Paul. "He was quite bare."

Aunt Isobel looked perturbed. "But he would have been cold," she pointed out.

"He had thick skin," explained Paul. "Like a twig."

"Like a twig?"

"Yes. You know that sort of wrinkly, nubbly skin on a twig."

Aunt Isobel knitted in silence for a second or two. She didn't like the little naked man nearly as much as the little

78

dressed man; she was trying to get used to him. After a while she went on.

"He lived in a bluebell wood, among the roots of a dear old tree. He had a dear little house, tunneled out of the soft, loamy earth, with a bright blue front door."

"Why didn't he live in it?" asked Paul.

"He did live in it, dear," exclaimed Aunt Isobel patiently.

"I thought he lived in the potting shed."

"In the potting shed?"

"Well, perhaps he had two houses. Some people do. I wish I'd seen the one with the blue front door."

"Did you see the one in the potting shed?" asked Aunt Isobel, after a second's bewildered silence.

"Not inside. Right inside. I'm too big. I just sort of saw into it with a flashlight."

"And what was it like?" asked Aunt Isobel, in spite of herself.

"Well, it was clean—in a potting-shed sort of way. He'd made the furniture himself. The floor was just earth but he'd trodden it down so that it was hard. It took him years."

"Well, dear, you seem to know more about him than I do."

Paul snuggled his head more comfortably against his elbow. He half-closed his eyes. "Go on," he said dreamily.

Aunt Isobel glanced at him hesitatingly. How beautiful he looked, she thought, lying there in the firelight with one curled hand lying lightly on the counterpane. "Well," she went on, "this little man had a little pipe made of a straw." She paused, rather pleased with this idea. "A little hollow straw, through which he played jiggity little tunes. And to which he danced." She hesitated. "Among the bluebells," she added. Really, this was quite a pretty story. She knitted hard for a few seconds, breathing heavily, before the next bit would come. "Now," she continued brightly, in a changed, higher, and more conversational voice, "up in the tree, there lived a fairy."

"In the tree?" asked Paul incredulously.

"Yes," said Aunt Isobel, "in the tree."

Paul raised his head. "Do you know that for certain?"

"Well, Paul," began Aunt Isobel. Then she added playfully, "Well, I suppose I do."

"Go on," said Paul.

"Well, this fairy—"

Paul raised his head again. "Couldn't you go on about the little man?"

"But, dear, we've done the little man—how he lived in the tree roots, and played a pipe, and all that."

"You didn't say about his hands and feet."

"His hands and feet?"

"How sort of big his hands and feet looked, and how he could scuttle along. Like a rat," Paul added.

"Like a rat!" exclaimed Aunt Isobel.

"And his voice. You didn't say anything about his voice."

"What sort of a voice," Aunt Isobel looked almost scared, "did he have?"

"A croaky sort of voice. Like a frog. And he says 'Will 'ee' and 'Do 'ee.'"

"Willy and Dooey . . ." repeated Aunt Isobel, as if fascinated.

"Instead of 'Will you' and 'Do you.' You know."

"Has he—got a Sussex accent?"

"Sort of. He isn't used to talking. He's the last one. He's been all alone, for years and years."

"Did he—" Aunt Isobel swallowed. "Did he tell you that?"

"Yes. He had an aunt and she died about fifteen years ago. But even when she was alive, he never spoke to her."

"Why?" asked Aunt Isobel.

"He didn't like her," said Paul.

There was silence. Paul stared dreamily into the fire. Aunt Isobel sat as if turned to stone, her hands idle in her lap. After a while, she cleared her throat. "When did you first see this little man, Paul?"

"Oh, ages and ages ago. When did you?"

"I— Where did you find him?"

"Under the chicken house."

"Did you—did you speak to him?"

Paul made a little snort. "No. I just popped a tin over him."

"You caught him!"

"Yes. There was an old rusty chicken food tin near. I just popped it over him." Paul laughed. "He scrabbled away inside. Then I popped an old kitchen plate that was there on top of the tin."

Aunt Isobel sat staring at Paul. "What—did you do with him then?"

"I put him in a cake tin, and made holes in the lid. I gave him a bit of bread and milk."

"Didn't he—say anything?"

"Well, he was sort of croaking."

"And then?"

"Well, I sort of forgot I had him."

"You forgot!"

"I went fishing, you see. Then it was bedtime. And next day I didn't remember him. Then when I went to look for him, he was lying curled up at the bottom of the tin. He'd gone all soft. He just hung over my finger. All soft."

Aunt Isobel's eyes protruded dully. "What did you do then?"

"I gave him some cherry cordial in a fountain pen filler."

"That revived him?"

"Yes, that's when he began to talk. And told me all about his aunt and everything. I harnessed him up, then, with a bit of string."

"Oh, Paul," exclaimed Aunt Isobel, "how cruel!"

"Well, he'd have got away. It didn't hurt him. Then I tamed him."

"How did you tame him?"

"Oh, how you tame anything. With food mostly. Chips of gelatine and raw sago he liked best. Cheese, he liked. I'd take him out and let him go down rabbit holes and things, on the string. Then he would come back and tell me what was going on. I put him down all kinds of holes in trees and things."

"Whatever for?"

"Just to know what was going on. I have all kinds of uses for him."

"Why," stammered Aunt Isobel, half rising from her chair, "you haven't still got him, have you?"

Paul sat up on his elbow. "Yes. I've got him. I'm going to keep him till I go to school. I'll need him at school like any-thing."

"But it isn't— You wouldn't be allowed—" Aunt Isobel became suddenly extremely grave. "Where is he now?"

"In the cake tin."

"Where is the cake tin?"

"Over there. In the toy cupboard."

Aunt Isobel looked fearfully across the shadowed room. She stood up. "I am going to put the light on, and I shall take that cake tin out into the garden."

"It's raining," Paul reminded her.

"I can't help that," said Aunt Isobel. "It is wrong and

wicked to keep a little thing like that shut up in a cake tin. I shall take it out on to the back porch and open the lid."

"He can hear you," said Paul.

"I don't care if he can hear me." Aunt Isobel walked toward the door. "I'm thinking of his good, as much as of anyone else's." She switched on the light. "Now, which was the cupboard?"

"That one, near the fireplace."

The door was ajar. Timidly Aunt Isobel pulled it open with one finger. There stood the cake tin amid a medley of torn cardboard, playing cards, pieces of jigsaw puzzle, and an open paint box.

"What a mess, Paul!"

Nervously Aunt Isobel stared at the cake tin and, falsely innocent, the British Royal Family stared back at her, painted brightly on a background of Allied flags. The holes in the lid were narrow and wedge-shaped; made, no doubt, by the big blade of the best cutting-out scissors.

Aunt Isobel drew in her breath sharply. "If you weren't ill, I'd make you do this. I'd make you carry the tin out and watch you open the lid—" She hesitated as if unnerved by the stillness of the rain-darkened room and the sinister quiet within the cake tin.

Then bravely she put out her hand. Paul watched her, absorbed, as she stretched forward the other hand and, very gingerly, picked up the cake tin. His eyes were dark and deep. He saw the lid was not quite on. He saw the corner, in contact with that ample bosom, rise. He saw the sharp edge catch the cord of Aunt Isobel's pince-nez and, fearing for her rimless glasses, he sat up in bed.

Aunt Isobel felt the tension, the pressure of the pince-nez on the bridge of her nose. A pull, it was, a little steady pull

83

as if a small dark claw, as wrinkled as a twig, had caught the hanging cord. . . .

"Look out!" cried Paul.

Loudly she shrieked and dropped the box. It bounced away and then lay still, gaping emptily upon its side. In the horrid hush, they heard the measured planking of the lid as it trundled off beneath the bed.

Paul broke the silence with a croupy cough. "Did you see him?" he asked, hoarse but interested.

"No," stammered Aunt Isobel, almost with a sob. "I didn't. I didn't see him."

"But you nearly did."

Aunt Isobel sat down limply in the upholstered chair. Her hand wavered vaguely round her brow and her cheeks looked white and pendulous, as if deflated. "Yes," she muttered, shivering slightly, "Heaven help me—I nearly did."

Paul gazed at her a moment longer. "That's what I mean," he said.

"What?" asked Aunt Isobel weakly, but as if she did not really care.

"About stories. Being real."

ALICE RUDOSKI

If Big Brother Says So

Margaret wondered if social workers *ever* shut up. Mrs. Gibbons hadn't stopped talking since they got in the car that morning to go to the new place. Now it was almost nighttime and they were still driving and she was still talking. It was boring always having to listen so you could say "yes" and "no" at the right time.

"You'll like Hattie McNabb, Margaret," Mrs. Gibbons was saying now, in her brisk, no-nonsense voice. "She has a small farm and there's only Hattie there, but you won't be lonesome. She loves children—she's got four grand-children, you know—and there are cats and little chickens. Doesn't that sound like fun?"

"Yes, Mrs. Gibbons," Margaret said.

Margaret was ten years old and had lived in eight different places. She knew what the place would be like. It would be no different from all the others. The lady would be nice while Mrs. Gibbons was there, but afterward she'd be mean, and Margaret wouldn't like that, and soon Mrs. Gibbons would come and take her away again.

Margaret stared at the road ahead. Her legs were getting stiff from being in the same position so long, and her back ached from sitting up straight. Besides, it was an old car, and the seats were hard. But she wasn't going to tell Mrs. Gibbons she was tired. She wasn't going to tell Mrs. Gibbons anything, not after she'd been so mean about Rodney. Margaret wished she could turn and talk to Rodney, but she knew Mrs. Gibbons wouldn't like that.

Margaret's thoughts were interrupted as Mrs. Gibbons shifted down and turned the car off the highway onto a narrow country road.

"Well, we're almost there," Mrs. Gibbons said. "Only another five miles or so and you'll see your new home." She paused, glancing at Margaret.

"Yes, Mrs. Gibbons," Margaret said.

"Now remember what you promised. You won't talk about—about silly things, will you?"

"No, Mrs. Gibbons."

"You're a big girl now, Margaret. You're too old for make-believe. And Mrs. McNabb said she'll find you some *real* friends."

"Yes, Mrs. Gibbons," Margaret said.

Mrs. Gibbons looked at Margaret, her lips tightening. "You certainly don't seem very excited," she said. "You could at least *try* to like it there."

Margaret's expression was cold and sullen but, for the first time since the trip started, she turned to Mrs. Gibbons as she answered her. "Maybe Rodney won't like it there," she said, slowly and deliberately.

Mrs. Gibbons gasped, and the car came to a jolting stop as she slammed on the brakes. "Rodney! Are you starting that foolishness again? What did I just tell you? And you know what the doctor said. There's no such person as Rodney, so stop that silly talk."

"Yes, Mrs. Gibbons," Margaret said, looking straight ahead again.

Mrs. Gibbons' hands were clenched on the steering wheel, her knuckles white. "I give up," she said. "What's the use?" She gave an exasperated sigh and turned her attention to the car.

Margaret was too tired to argue, and she wasn't going to even think about what that stupid doctor had said. Rodney was her big brother, and he looked after her, no matter what everyone else said. Mrs. Gibbons would sure get a surprise if she knew that Rodney was sitting right beside Margaret. Didn't she wonder why Margaret had to sit so close to the door?

Margaret almost smiled when she thought about how Mrs. Gibbons would jump if Rodney said something to her. Except that Rodney didn't talk. When anyone was mean to Margaret and she told Rodney about it, he just smiled and nodded, and made sure that no one was mean to her again. He took good care of her.

Margaret suddenly realized that the car wasn't moving. The motor was running but they were still stopped on that old road, and it was getting dark outside.

Mrs. Gibbons was wrenching at the gear shift, annoyed and flustered. "Now what's the matter with this old car?" she muttered.

"Yes, Mrs. Gibbons," Margaret said, not certain what she had heard, but sure that she was supposed to be listening.

"Yes, Mrs. Gibbons, no, Mrs. Gibbons," Mrs. Gibbons echoed, her patience suddenly gone. "Can't you say anything else? If it hadn't been for you we wouldn't be in this predicament now—you and that idiot Rodney you dreamed up. Now the gears are locked and I haven't even got a flashlight."

She got out of the car, slamming the door as she left, and went around to the front to lift the hood and peer into the maze underneath.

Margaret sat quietly, thinking about what Mrs. Gibbons had said. Rodney was not an idiot. If it hadn't been for him, Margaret would still be at the last place with that little brat, Benny. And Benny wasn't there anymore either. He was always kicking and hitting and when Margaret finally hit him back, she got spanked and sent to her room.

No one listened when she said that Benny had been mean to her. So she told Rodney. He smiled, nodded, and the next day Benny fell down the stairs and died, and Mrs. Gibbons came to take Margaret to the new place. Margaret was lucky she had a big brother to take care of her.

Mrs. Gibbons had come around to Margaret's side of the car and opened the door. She reached in, grabbed Margaret by the shoulders, and shook her. "Will you please pay attention? I've called you three times. You have to help me with this car."

"Yes, Mrs. Gibbons," Margaret said, her shoulders hurting from the rough fingers.

"Move over, closer to the steering wheel. Can you reach that pedal? There—that's the one."

Margaret nodded.

"Now keep your foot down on that pedal until I tell you to take it away. I don't want to stop the motor in case I have trouble with that, too. But when I unlock the gears, the car could move if you don't hold that pedal down. Do you understand?"

Without waiting for an answer, Mrs. Gibbons closed the door and went back to work on the gear shift.

Margaret sat awkwardly, her foot pressed hard on the brake pedal. For a long time she watched the faint lights of a farmhouse in the distance, wondering if they were the lights of her new home. Once, above the sound of the car motor, she could hear rattling noises coming from under the hood where Mrs. Gibbons was trying to fix the car. She thought of Mrs. Gibbons, and her shoulders hurt. She told Rodney about it. That made them feel better, but her leg was getting tired.

Margaret wished she could drive a car, and then she'd push on the gas and drive to someplace where no one would ever be mean to her again. She would live with Rodney and he would take care of her.

She heard a clicking sound, and then Mrs. Gibbons was a silhouette against the sky as she reached up to close the hood. Margaret wondered if Rodney could drive a car. Rodney smiled and nodded.

JOYCE CARY

A Private Ghost

As soon as he awoke in the morning, Peter, aged eight, felt a difference. Then he remembered that his father and mother were away—they had gone to Dublin very suddenly for the weekend—and that Grandaunt was also away. His grandaunt lived close by, and always when his parents had been away she had come to stay and watch over the children. But now she was in a Dublin hospital. No one had come to hear his prayers last night. This was why, he thought, he felt a difference.

His sister Noni, in the next bed, did not notice a difference. As soon as she awoke, she proposed to come into his bed, as usual; but he refused her firmly. He was devoted to Noni, and she adored him, but at the moment he did not want adoration. He was preoccupied, listening intently to the household. Noni at six was too young to notice the difference.

Certainly, the household *was* different. It was so different that he could hardly recognize it. The cat next door in the

90

day nursery was meowing loudly in a despairing voice; it had not been let out yet. Down in the kitchen, below the night nursery window, someone with a very deep hoarse voice, some old beggar, perhaps, was talking to a dog. And this strange dog was padding round the floor, rattling its claws on the linoleum, and uttering now and then a little whine.

What was stranger still on this strange day was that when Annie the nurse came in five minutes later to get the children up, Lizzie the housemaid came with her. Lizzie and Annie had not been speaking for weeks past. But now they came in laughing, and Lizzie whispered something. Then she ran out of the nursery and shouted down the well of the stairs to the cook, "I told Annie on you, Maggie." Even her voice was a new voice, more like Maggie's when she was drunk. But Lizzie didn't drink.

Breakfast in the day nursery was delayed, and Noni grew impatient. She climbed into her chair and beat on the table with a spoon. Annie, however, was down in the kitchen telling some tale to the beggar, and what was still queerer, she had left the nursery doors wide open. The nurseries, usually so jealously kept aloof, now seemed as public as the back stairs, through which all these peculiar noises were piped direct to the children. Peter sat at the table listening. He frowned. He did not like the difference in the house. He felt a certain nervousness, and he also felt a certain responsibility, but for what, he did not know.

Suddenly he took the spoon out of Noni's hand and said, "Don't do that—it's rude." This was unexpected to Noni. Peter was usually kind to her. She flushed with pain and surprise. Her forehead crinkled and the corners of her mouth turned down; she was about to cry. But Peter's glance daunted her. He said severely, "You're not a baby anymore."

Lizzie came in again when Annie brought the tray. The two were giggling together again at something that had happened in the kitchen. And then Lizzie shouted from the window at Mrs. Conor, the gardener's wife, slopping past in the rain with a sack over her head and her skirt turned up to the knees. Mrs. Conor answered with cheerful yells, and soon she, too, came up to the nursery. She spent the whole morning there, drinking tea and telling stories that made the usually dignified Annie explode through her nose with protesting cries, "Oh, Mrs. Conor, you're killing me!"

Mrs. Conor stayed all day. After the children's dinner, at noon, all the staff gathered in the day nursery, and there was great laughter when Lizzie was persuaded to ride the rocking-horse—not that Lizzie needed much persuading. She was a pale, high-breasted girl, with big gray eyes and a little round mouth, who was mad about dancing, and even when the family were there she would go bouncing through the rooms as if she were late for a ball. When she was on the horse, she laughed so much that she nearly fell off. Then Maggie pushed the horse to make it rock harder, and Lizzie gave a shriek like an engine and began to be angry. But when they all laughed she stopped being angry and proposed a dance.

So Annie played the gramophone. They did not dance, however; they were tired of the idea already. And they began to make much of the children. All of them were devoted to Peter and Noni, and now in the exuberance of their holiday, they were demonstrative, they competed in affection. Lizzie tickled Noni till she laughed herself crimson, and this almost provoked a scene. For Annie, the nurse, taken suddenly jealous, snatched the child away and said, "That's enough." Lizzie turned upon her and laughed in her nose, saying, "You, Annie—" At that moment, Mrs. Conor, the hanger-on, who was not quite of the inner household but earned her cups of tea by her good stories and her flattery, made a quick diversion. She lifted Peter to her lap and stroked his hair, which was as pale as flax. "Oh, the pet—the spit of his grandda. And do you know, my prince, that I've seen him? I've seen your grandda with my own eyes."

The maids gazed at her. Annie's breast was still heaving, and Lizzie's little mouth was still pushed out in scorn, but they were attentive. They knew that Mrs. Conor had some trick in hand.

"Come now, Mrs. Conor," said Annie in her downright way. "The old master is dead this forty years."

"Wasn't that the one that drowned himself in the river?" Lizzie asked.

"Forty-three years," said Mrs. Conor, "and that was before I was born, but I've seen him." And looking at the child, she said to him, "And how do you think that was, my pet? How do you think I saw him that was dead?" Peter gazed earnestly at Mrs. Conor, and Noni, who had come to lean against her brother, made big eyes around his arm. They knew the question was not meant to be answered; it was simply an introduction to Mrs. Conor's story. "It was when I was eight—just your age, my pet—that I saw him walk. He was all in white, and while he walked he kept shaking his hands and the water was dripping from him. And, bless you, I didn't know who he was then, or what it meant. But I was frightened, and I ran to my mother, and it was then she told me about the old master. And she said if I was to see him again I must cross myself."

93

There was a short silence. All four of the servants were gazing at the two children to see the effect of this tale.

"And they say," said Mrs. Conor, "they say that it's only a child has ever seen the old master walk."

"Was it a ghost?" Noni asked in a loud voice.

"Yes, indeed. You wouldn't see him living when he was dead, would you, pet?"

"Ghosts are only stories," Noni said. "Pappy told me."

Peter opened his mouth to say the same thing. But as he glanced up he caught the maids' eyes fixed upon him, and suddenly he was not so sure that they were playing a trick upon him. When Annie or Maggie codded him about potatoes that grew on trees or the man in the moon, they had a laugh in them. They might look grave, but you could feel the laugh. But now there was no laugh, and their grave faces had a different gravity. All at once, he was not as confident of his father's assurances, even about ghosts. Did his father know that things could be so different at home when he was away?

"There aren't such things," Noni said indignantly. But Peter looked at her severely, and she turned red.

"Well, now," Mrs. Conor said, "do you tell me I'm telling you lies?"

The children looked at her, and Peter said, "Grandda fell in when he was fishing."

"I wouldn't know that," Mrs. Conor said. "But if he only fell in, why would he walk?"

"Why, indeed?" Lizzie said. "And why only for children?"

"Well now," Mrs. Conor said, "I wouldn't know that either, but isn't it the same with the fairies? They say it's only children and naturals can see the wee folk. And so you never saw the like of him, Master Peter?"

Peter shook his head, and Mrs. Conor looked around at

her audience. "If anyone were to see the old master, it would be this one that's so like him." And suddenly she winked. Mrs. Conor was a good winker; she could close either eye without the slightest change of expression on the other side of her face. That's why Peter saw only her grave good-natured countenance, while Maggie and Lizzie and Annie had a glimpse of enormous slyness. Mrs. Conor once more turned her grave mild face toward Peter. "Yes, my dear, you would be the one, for aren't you the spit of him? It's a wonder that you haven't seen him yet, for it's my belief he crosses that backyard every day of the week on his way from the water to the cemetery."

"What, Mrs. Conor?" Lizzie said. "Every day of the week? I wouldn't like to think that."

"No, indeed," said Maggie, coming into the game. Maggie was old and tired, and slow in her mind, but still she was ready to take her part in a good game. "No, indeed," she said. "Why, I'd be afraid to go into the yard if I thought that."

"But then you wouldn't see him," Annie said. "It would be only Master Peter here that would see him."

"It was about six o'clock in the evening that I saw him," said Mrs. Conor. "And they said that was the time that he went into the water."

There was another long pause, and then Lizzie said, "Well, now, I wonder, would Master Peter see him if he looked at six o'clock?"

"It'd be a bit dark at six," Maggie said.

"It'd have to be," said Mrs. Conor. "You don't think that ghosts will walk in daylight? But there, I'm not saying that Master Peter would see his grandda on any day of the week, dark as it might be."

95

"No," Maggie said. "It's only that he might take a look some evening if he wouldn't be afraid."

"It's well he might be," Lizzie said. She gave a deep sigh and gazed into the air with her big gray eyes, imagining the terror of ghosts.

"He would not!" Annie cried. "Would you, my darling? Would you now?"

Peter made no answer to this. He understood the challenge. He had been challenged before, and usually in a trick, as when Maggie had dared him to open a parcel, which, so she said, might have a bomb in it, and it had let out a jumping jack, which hit him on the nose. But he had not really believed that there would be a bomb in a parcel. Who would put bombs in parcels? Ghosts were quite another thing. And it was true that his grandfather had died young, and tragically.

"Oh, he's the brave boy always," Mrs. Conor said, and Maggie came in hastily, "Sure. There never was any of the family afraid of anything."

"Would you look for your grandda?" Lizzie asked, staring at the boy with her big eyes.

Peter, staring back and wondering at this strange excited Lizzie, answered, "You mean in the yard?"

"You wouldn't have to go in the yard," said Mrs. Conor. "You could see from the kitchen window. Aye, it would be better from the window."

"And what better day than today, when themselves is out of it?" Lizzie said.

"It's stopped raining," Peter said, as if he had not noticed Lizzie's suggestion. "Can I go to Willy?" Willy was the garden boy, a close friend of Peter's, but Annie did not always approve of their meetings which, she considered, were often too exciting for Peter and kept him awake at night.

"There now," Lizzie muttered. "I knew he'd get out of it."

"Of course you can go to Willy," Mrs. Conor said quickly. "He'd be in the cabbages this minute. And I tell you, why wouldn't ye have supper in the kitchen, too—for a treat? I'm sure Annie wouldn't mind just for today."

"Oh, yes!" cried Noni. "Oh, yes, yes please."

And even Peter, disturbed as he was by the confusion in the house, was pleased by this suggestion. "Oh, do, Annie. I'd like that very much," he said.

"Sure, my pet," Annie said.

"Indeed, and ye shall," said Maggie, winking at Mrs. Conor, but so clumsily that Noni noticed and stared at her eye. Maggie was very red, and seemed about to burst.

"And as for ghosts, Miss Noni," said Mrs. Conor, "sure your pappy may be right after all. Why, I wouldn't be too sure myself. It's so long since I saw one that indeed your grandda mightn't have been one at all. There now, Maggie, don't I hear your kettle?" And the four rushed suddenly out of the room so violently that they jammed on the narrow back stairs and Lizzie gave a squeak of laughter. Then, below, the kitchen door banged shut behind them.

Peter paid no more attention to their nonsense. He was too pleased with himself for eluding Mrs. Conor's embarrassing proposal. Joyfully he hurried off to see Willy in the garden. He even allowed Noni to take his hand and go with him, stipulating only that she should not speak to Willy.

Noni was perfectly satisfied to be beside her darling and listen to his conversation with Willy, while the party moved from the cabbages to the byre, the byre to the pigsty, the pigsty to the pump, where Willy completed his last duty by filling the house tanks, so that, as he said thoughtfully, "You wains can have your baths the night."

Peter provided most of the talk, giving, for instance, a full

97

account of the mammoth found in Russia under the ice and explaining that whales were really animals, and had milk. He hadn't had so good a day with Willy for a week, and he started back to the kitchen in the highest spirits. The reason the children loved supper in the kitchen was that the maids, and especially Lizzie, were such good company with their gossip and their jokes. They were always playing some trick on each other and laughing. Last time, Lizzie had pulled Annie's chair away and caused her to sit down hard on the floor. The children had laughed until they could not eat, and Lizzie herself had had to say that they must behave themselves better or they would not be asked again.

They were laughing in recollection of this performance when they came into the kitchen. But what a surprise! There was no one there but old Maggie, and the table was not by the stove, but pushed into the window embrasure, close against the window itself. And when Maggie had placed them in their chairs, at opposite ends of the table, she made for the door.

"Oh, Maggie," Noni wailed, "I want to have supper with you all." But Maggie muttered something about the storeroom, and went out, shutting the door after her.

Almost at the same moment, there was a moaning cry from the yard, and Peter, who had been put facing the yard gate that led from the front lawn and the river, looked up and saw the ghost. It was just coming through the gate.

The lamp in the kitchen was turned low, and the yard was lit only by the sky, which was a pale green color. The yard, surrounded by barns and stables, by the byre and garage, all in dark reddish bricks, was paved with dark blue cinders; these dark buildings and the dark cinders soaked up the light from above. The air in the yard seemed to be without light, so that the whiteness of the ghost was as bright as a swan's feathers on a dark evening. The ghost was all in white; a short thick figure in a sheet, which was pulled over its forehead in front, and which covered its body and fell to the ground so that the creature did not seem to have feet.

When it passed the gardener's shed, it turned toward the kitchen window. And now Peter could see, under the white fold of the sheet, a face as white, except that its eyes were like enormous black holes, and its mouth was gray. This mouth was moving all the time as if crying.

Peter was fixed in such fear, such horror, that he could not take his eyes off this face with its weeping mouth. He got down slowly from his chair and retreated a pace backwards; but this brought him up against the end of the embrasure. And he stood there, fixed, helpless, unable to move, speak, or think.

"What are you doing, Peter?" Noni said, surprised at his getting down from his chair. Then the ghost moaned again, more loudly. Noni looked around, gave a shriek, and ran to her brother. Peter held her tight and drew her to one side—she hid her face against his ribs.

The ghost was now four or five yards from the window. Peter could see long leaves of river weed glistening wet on its shoulders and the water pouring down the white folds to the ground—the eyes were shining palely in the middle of their great black holes. It was staring at him and shaking its hands all the time as if in grief. He thought, "It's crying—it wants to tell me something." He was shivering in terror that the creature would speak to him, and yet he could not run away. He felt he had to wait for the message.

The ghost took one more step toward him and gave another long deep heartbreaking moan. Noni gripped Peter convulsively and uttered shriek after shriek. But the ghost's next move was to its right. With a wavering, wobbling motion, it glided slowly toward the back corner of the house, where it suddenly vanished behind the porch of the scullery.

Almost at the same moment, Annie, Lizzie, and Maggie burst into the kitchen. Peter, mechanically patting and stroking Noni, gazed at them with wide vague eyes as if he had forgotten their existence. Noni stopped screaming and ran toward Annie. "It came—it came—we saw it!" she cried. But the maids were staring at Peter, with eyes nearly as wide as his own—half curious, half alarmed at the child's fearfully white face and crazy expression.

"What—what happened then?" said Annie in a stammering voice.

And now Mrs. Conor, rather breathless, came darting into the kitchen from the scullery. She still had some burnt cork under her right eye, but she covered it with her hand, so that the children could not see it. "What's wrong?" she said. "Was that Miss Noni I heard?"

"They saw him, Mrs. Conor!" Lizzie exclaimed. "They saw the old master in the yard—did you ever hear the like of that?"

Peter came to himself, walked out of his corner, and took Noni's hand. "It was nothing," he said. And his face turned very red.

"A ghost, nothing?" said Mrs. Conor. "Weren't you afeared?"

"We didn't see anything," he said. "It was only Noni being silly. You didn't see anything, did you, Noni?"

Noni stared at him. Then she slowly shook her head. She didn't know why Peter was telling this enormous lie, but she was glad to support him.

He then walked her slowly and with great dignity toward the hall door. The maids parted and let him go. Even Mrs.

100

Conor was taken aback by this strangely aloof Peter. He led Noni through the hall into the drawing room. He seldom went to the drawing room except on state occasions, in his best clothes. For him, it was a place of ceremony, where grown-up persons of distinction conferred together in quiet tones and a reserved manner upon important matters—births, deaths, marriages, money, family affairs.

As soon as they entered the room, Noni protested that it was a ghost. "I *saw* it." Peter shut the door firmly behind them and cut off the excited chatter of the maids. Then he led Noni to the middle of the carpet and explained to her, kindly but gravely, "Yes, it was grandpapa. But don't talk to them about it. They'd only laugh and he's our own grandpapa."

RAY BRADBURY

The
Playground

H e had often walked by the playground on the way
from his train and paid it no particular attention. He
neither liked nor disliked it, he had no opinion of it.
But his wife had looked at him across the breakfast table
this morning and said, "I'm going to start Jim at the playground this week. You know, the one down the street. Jim's
old enough now."

At his office, Mr. Charles Underhill had made a memo-
randum: *Look at playground.* And on the way home down the
street from the train at four in the afternoon, he purposely
folded his newspaper so he would not read himself past the
playground.

Now, at four-ten in the late day, he moved slowly along
the sidewalk and stopped at the playground gate.

At first there was nothing. And then, as his ears adjusted
outward from his usual interior monologues, it was like
turning the volume dial of a radio louder. And the scene
before him, like a gray, blurred television image, came to a

slow focus. Primarily, there were faint voices, faint cries, streaks and shadows, vague impressions. And then, as if someone had jolted the machine, there were screams, sharp visions, children dashing, children fighting, pummeling, bleeding, screaming! He saw the tiniest scabs on their faces and knees in amazing clarity.

Mr. Underhill stood there in the full volume of blasting sound, blinking. And then his nostrils took up where his eyes and ears left off.

He smelled the cutting odors of iodine, raw adhesive, and pink Mercurochrome, so strong it was bitter to his tongue. The wind of iodine moving through the steely wire fence which glinted dully in the gray light of the overcast day. And the rushing children there, it was like hell cut loose in a great pinball machine, a colliding and banging and totaling of hits and pushes and rushes to a grand and as yet unforseen total of brutalities. And was he mistaken or was the light of a strange intensity within the playground; everything seeming to possess four shadows, one dark one, and three subsidiaries, which made it impossible, strategically, to tell which way the small bodies were screaming until they bashed their targets. Yes, the oblique, pressing light made the entire playground seem deep, far away, and somehow remote from his touching it. Or perhaps it was the hard steel wire fence, not unlike certain park zoo barriers, beyond which anything might happen.

"A pen of misery, that's what it is," said Mr. Underhill. "Why do children insist on making life miserable for each other? It's nothing but torture to be a child." He heard himself give a great relieved sigh. Thank God, childhood was over and done for him. No more pinchings, bruisings, shattered dreams, and senseless excitements.

A gust of wind tore the paper from his hand and blew it

through the gate. He went after it, down into the playground, three steps. Clutching it, he immediately retreated, heart pounding, for in the moment he had remained stranded in the playground's atmosphere he had felt his hat too large, his coat too cumbersome, his belt too loose, his shoes too big, he had felt like a small boy playing businessman in his father's clothes, and the gate behind him had loomed impossibly large, while the sky itself pressed grayer at his eyes, and the scent of the iodine, like that of a feral tiger's mouth exhaled upon him, touched and blew his hair. He almost stumbled and fell, getting out of there!

He stood outside, like someone who has just emerged, shocked, from a terrible, cold sea.

"Hello, Charlie!"

He heard the voice and turned to see who had called him. There was the caller, on top a slide, a boy about nine years old, waving. "Hello, Charlie!"

Mr. Charles Underhill raised a hand. "But I don't *know* that boy," he murmured. "And why should he call me by my first name?"

The boy was smiling up in the murky air, and now, jostled by other yelling children, rushed shrieking down the slide.

Mr. Underhill stood bemused by what he saw. Now the playground was an immense iron industry whose sole product was pain, sorrow, and sadism. If you stood here half an hour there wasn't a face in the entire enclosure that didn't wince, cry, redden with anger, or pale with fear, one minute or another. Really! Who said childhood was the best time of life, when in reality it was the most horrifying, the most merciless era, the barbaric time when there were no police to protect you, only parents preoccupied with themselves and the taller world. No, if he had his way, he gripped the

fence with one fist, they'd nail a new sign here: TOR-
QUEMADA'S GREEN.

And as for that boy, the one who had shouted at him,
who was he? There was something familiar there, perhaps
in the hidden bones, an echo of some old friend, probably
the son of a successfully ulcered father.

And this is the playground where my son will play,
thought Mr. Underhill, and shuddered.

Hanging his hat in the hall, checking his lean image in the
watery mirror, Mr. Underhill felt wintry and tired. When
his wife appeared, and his son came tapping on mousefeet,
he greeted them with something less than full attention.
The boy clambered thinly over him, playing "King of the
hill." And the father, fixing his gaze to the end of the cigar
he was slowly lighting, finally cleared his throat and said,
"I've been thinking about that playground, Susan."

"I'm taking Jim over tomorrow," said his wife.

"Not really? *That* playground?"

His mind rebelled. The smell and look of the place were
still vivid to him. That writhing world with its atmosphere
of cuts and beaten noses, the air as full of pain as a dentist's
office, and those horrid tic-tac-toes and hopscotches under
his feet as he picked up his newspaper, horrid for no reason
he could see!

"What's wrong with that playground?" asked his wife.

"Have you seen it?" He paused in confusion. "Damn it, I
mean, the children there. It's a Black Hole, that's what it is."

"The children are clean and from well-to-do families."

"Why, they shove and push like vulgar little Gestapos,"
cried Mr. Underhill. "It'd be like shoving the child in a gra-
nary to be ground down into meal by a couple of two-ton

105

grinders! Every time I think of Jim settling into that bar-baric pit, I turn cold!"

"You know it's the only convenient center."

"They'll kill Jim. I saw some with all kinds of bats and clubs and guns. Good God, Jim'll be in splinters by the end of the first day. They'll have him on a spit with an orange in his mouth."

"How you exaggerate!" She was laughing at him.

"I'm serious!"

"You can't live Jim's life for him, you know that. He has to learn the hard way. He's got to be beat up and beat others up; children are like that."

"I don't *like* children like that."

"It's the happiest time of life."

"Nonsense! I used to look back on childhood with nostalgia. Now I realize I was a sentimental fool. It was nothing but scratching and beating and kicking and coming home a bleeding scab from head to foot. If I could possibly save Jim from that, I would."

"That's impractical and anyway, thank God, impossible."

"I won't have him near that place, I tell you. I'll have him grow up a neurotic recluse first."

"Charlie!"

"I will! Those little beasts, you should've *seen* them! He's my only son, Jim is." He felt the boy's skinny legs about his shoulders, the boy's delicate hands rumpling his hair. "I won't have him butchered."

"He'll get it in school, later. Better to let him get a little shoving about now, when he's three, so he's prepared for it."

"I've thought of that, too." Mr. Underhill fiercely held to his son's ankles that dangled like warm, thin sausages on either lapel. "I might even get a private tutor for him!"

"Oh, Charles!"

They did not speak during dinner.

After dinner, he took Jim for a walk while his wife was washing the dishes. They strolled down past the playground under the dim street lamps. It was a cooling September night, with the first sniff of autumn in it. Next week, and the children would be raked in off the fields like so many leaves and set to burning in the schools, using their fire and energy for more constructive purposes. But they would be here after school, ramming about, making projectiles of themselves, exploding and crashing, leaving a wake of misery behind their miniature wars.

"Wanna go in," said Jim, leaning against the cold wire fence, watching the horrible children beat each other and run.

"No, Jim, you don't want that."

"Play," said Jim, his eyes glassy with fascination, as he saw a large boy kick a small boy and the small boy kick a smaller boy to even things up.

"Play, Daddy."

"Come along, Jim, you'll never get in that mess if *I* can help it." Mr. Underhill tugged the small arm firmly.

"Play." Jim was beginning to blubber now. His eyes were melting out of his cheeks. His face became a wrinkled orange of color and feeling.

Some of the children heard the crying and glanced over. Underhill had the terrible sense of watching a den of foxes suddenly startled and looked up from the white hairy ruin of a dead rabbit. The mean yellow eyes, the conical chins, the white teeth, the dreadful wiry hair, the brambly sweaters, the iron-colored hands covered with a day's battle dust.

They saw Jim and he was new. They didn't say anything, but as Jim cried louder and Mr. Underhill, by main force, dragged him like a cement bag along the walk, they watched the little boy. Mr. Underhill felt like pushing his fist at them and crying, "You little beasts, you won't get *my* son!"

And then, with beautiful irrelevance, the boy at the top of the slide, the boy with the familiar face, called to him, waving.

"Hello, Charlie."

Mr. Underhill paused and Jim stopped crying.

"See you later, Charlie."

And the face of the boy way up there on that high slide, was suddenly like the face of Thomas Marshall, an old business friend who lived just around the block but whom he hadn't seen in years.

"See you later, Charlie."

Later, later? What did the fool boy mean?

"I know *you,* Charlie!" called the boy. "Hi!"

"What?" gasped Mr. Underhill.

"Tomorrow night, Charlie, hey!" And the boy fell off the slide and lay choking for breath, face like a cheese from the fall, while children jumped on him and tumbled over.

Mr. Underhill stood undecided for five seconds or more, until Jim thought to cry again and then, with the fox eyes upon them, in the first chill of autumn, he dragged Jim all the way home.

The next afternoon Mr. Underhill finished at the office early and took the three o'clock train, arriving out in Green Town at three-twenty-five, in plenty of time to drink in the brisk rays of the autumnal sun. Strange how one day it is suddenly autumn, he thought. One day it is summer and the next, how could you measure or tell it? Something about the temperature or smell? Or the sediment of age knocked loose from your bones during the night and circulating in your blood and heart, giving you a slight tremble and a chill? A year older, a year dying, was *that* it?

He walked up toward the playground, planning the future. It seemed you did more planning in autumn than any other season. This had to do with dying, perhaps. You thought of death and you automatically planned. Well, then, there was to be a tutor for Jim *that* was positive; none of those horrible schools for him. It would pinch the bank account a bit, but Jim would at least grow up a happy boy. They would pick and choose his friends. Any slambang bullies would be thrown out as soon as they so much as touched Jim. And as for this playground. Completely out of the question!

"Oh, hello, Charles."

He looked up suddenly. Before him, at the entrance to the wire enclosure, stood his wife. He noted instantly that she called him Charles, instead of Dear. Last night's unpleasantness had not quite evaporated. "Susan, what're you doing down here?"

She flushed guiltily and glanced in through the fence.

"You didn't!" he cried.

His eyes sought among the scrabbling, running, screaming children. "Do you mean to say . . . ?"

His wife nodded, half amused. "I thought I'd bring him early—"

"Before I got home, so I wouldn't know is *that* it?"

That was it.

"Good God, Susan, where *is* he?"

"I just came to see."

"You mean you left him there all afternoon?"

"Just half an hour while I shopped."

"And you *left* him, good God!" Mr. Underhill flung his

109

hand to his drained cheek. "Well, come on, find him, get him out of there!"

They peered in together past the wire to where some boys charged about, to girls slapping each other, to a squabbling heap of children who seemed to take turns at getting off, taking a good run, and jumping one against another.

"That's where he is, I *know* it!" said Mr. Underhill.

Just then, across the field at full speed, sobbing and wailing, came Jim, with six boys after him. He fell, got up, ran, fell again, stumbled up, shrieking, and the boys behind him shot beans through metal shooters.

"I'll stuff those blowers up their noses!" cried Mr. Underhill. "Come on, Jim! Run!"

Jim made it to the gate. Mr. Underhill caught him and it was like catching a rumpled, bloody wad of material. Jim's nose was bleeding and his pants were ripped and he was covered with grime.

"There's your playground," said Mr. Underhill, bent to his knees, staring up from his son, patting him, to his wife, viciously. "There's your sweet happy little innocents, your well-to-do piddling Fascists! Let me catch this boy in there again and there'll be hell. Come on, Jim. All right, you little bastards, get back there!" he shouted.

"We didn't do nothing," said the children.

"What's the world coming to?" Mr. Underhill questioned the universe.

"Hi, Charlie," said the strange boy, standing to one side. He waved casually and smiled.

"Who's that?" asked Susan.

"How in hell do *I* know?" snapped Mr. Underhill.

"Be seeing you, Charlie, so long," called the boy.

Mr. Underhill marched his wife and child home.

"Take your hand off my elbow!" she said.

He was trembling, absolutely, continually trembling with rage when he got to bed. He had tried some coffee, but nothing stopped it. He wanted to beat their pulpy little brains out, those gross Cruikshank children; yes, that phrase fit them, those fox-fiend, melancholy Cruikshank children, with all the guile and poison and slyness in their cold faces. In the name of all that was decent, what manner of child was this new generation? A bunch of cutters and hangers and kickers, a drove of bleeding, moronic thumb-screwers, with the sewage of neglect running in their veins? He lay violently jerking his head from one side of his hot pillow to the other, and at last got up and lit a cigarette, but it wasn't enough. He and Susan had had a huge battle when they got home. He had yelled at her and she had yelled back, peacock and peahen shrieking in a wilderness where law and order were insanities laughed at and forgotten.

He was ashamed. You didn't fight violence with violence, not if you were a gentleman. You talked calmly. But she didn't give him a chance, damn it! She wanted the boy put in a vice and squashed. She wanted him reamed and punctured and given the laying-on-of-hands. To be beaten from playground to kindergarten, to grammar school, to junior high, to high school. If he was lucky, in high school, the beatings and sadisms would refine themselves, the sea of blood and spittle would drain back down the shore of years and Jim would be left upon the edge of maturity, with God knows what outlook to the future, with a desire, perhaps, to be a wolf among wolves, a dog among dogs, a fiend among fiends. But there was enough of that in the world, already. And the very thought of the next ten or fifteen years of torture was enough to make Mr. Underhill cringe, he felt his own flesh impaled with a BB shot, stung, burned, fisted, scrounged, twisted, violated, and bruised. He quivered, like a jellyfish hurled violently into a concrete mixer. Jim would never survive it. Jim was too delicate for this horror.

"I've made up my mind," said Susan, in bed. "You needn't walk the room all night. Jim's not having a private tutor. He's going to school. And he's going back to that playground tomorrow and keep going back until he's learned to stand on his own two feet."

"Let me alone." Mr. Underhill dressed. Downstairs, he opened the front door. It was about five minutes to midnight as he walked swiftly down the street, trying to outdistance his rage and outrage. He knew Susan was right, of course. This was the world, you lived in it, you accepted it, but *that* was the very trouble! He had been through the mill already, he knew what it was to be a boy among lions, his own childhood had come rushing back to him the last few hours, a time of terror and violence, and now he could not bear to think of Jim going through it all, those long years, especially if you were a delicate child, through no fault of your own, your bones thin, your face pale, what could you expect but to be harried and chased?

He stopped by the playground which was still lit by one great overhead lamp. It was locked for the night, but that one light remained on until twelve. He wanted to tear the contemptible place down, rip up the steel fences, obliterate the slides, and say to the children, "Go home! Play in your backyards!"

How ingenious, the cold, deep playground. You never knew where anyone lived. The boy who knocked your teeth out, who was *he*? Nobody knew. Where did he live? Nobody knew. How to find him? Nobody knew. Why, you could come here one day, beat the living tar out of some smaller child, and run on the next day to some *other* playground. They would never find you. From playground to playground, you could take your criminal tricks, with everyone forgetting you, since they never knew you. You could return to this playground a month later, and if the little child whose teeth you knocked out was there and recognized you, you could deny it. No, I'm not the one. Must be some other kid. This is my first time here! No, not me! And when his back is turned, knock him down. And run off down the nameless streets, a nameless person.

"What am I going to do?" asked Mr. Underhill. "I can't buck Susan forever on this. Should we move to the country? I can't do that. But I can't have Jim here, either."

"Hello, Charlie," said a voice.

Mr. Underhill turned. Inside the fence, seated in the dirt, making diagrams with one finger in the cold dust, was the nine-year-old boy. He didn't look up. He said hello, Charlie, just sitting there, easily, in that world beyond the hard steel fence.

Mr. Underhill said, "How do you know my name?"

"You're having a lot of trouble." The boy crossed his legs comfortably, smiling.

"How'd you get in there so late? Who are you?"

"My name's Marshall—"

"Of course, Tom Marshall's son. Tommy. I *thought* you looked familiar."

"More familiar than you think." The boy laughed.

"How's your father, Tommy?"

"Have you seen him lately?" the boy asked.

"Briefly, on the street, a month ago."

"How did he look?"

"What?"

"How did Mr. Marshall look?" asked the boy. It was strange he wouldn't say "my father."

"He looked all right. Why?"

113

"I guess he's happy," said the boy. Mr. Underhill saw the boy's arms and legs and they were covered with scabs and scratches.

"Aren't you going home, Tommy?"

"I sneaked out to see you. I just knew you'd come. You're afraid."

Mr. Underhill didn't know what to say.

"Those little monsters," he said at last.

"Maybe I can help you." The boy made a dust triangle. It was ridiculous. "How?"

"You'd give anything, wouldn't you, if you could spare Jim all this? You'd trade places with him if you could?"

Mr. Underhill nodded, frozen.

"Well, you come down here tomorrow afternoon at four. Then I can help you."

"How do you mean, help?"

"I can't tell you outright," said the boy. "It has to do with the playground. Any place where there's lots of evil, that makes power. You can feel it, can't you?"

A kind of warm wind stirred off the bare field under the one high light. Underhill shivered. Yes, even now, at midnight, the playground was evil, for it was used for evil things. "Are all playgrounds like this?"

"Some. Maybe this is the only one like this. What I wanted to say is that Tom Marshall was like you. He worried about Tommy Marshall and the playground and the kids, too. He wanted to save Tommy the trouble and the hurt, also."

This business of talking about people as if they were remote, made Mr. Underhill feel like laughing.

"So we made a bargain," said the boy.

"Who with?"

"With the playground, I guess, or whoever runs it."

"Who runs it?"

"I've never seen him. There's an office over there under the grandstand. A light burns in it all night. It's a bright, blue light, kind of funny. There's a desk there with no papers on it and an empty chair. The sign says Manager, but nobody ever sees the man."

"He must be around."

"That's right," said the boy. "Or I wouldn't be where I am, and someone else wouldn't be where they are."

"You certainly talk grown-up."

The boy was pleased. "Want to know who I really am? I'm not Tommy Marshall. I'm Tom Marshall, the father. I know you won't believe it. But I was afraid for Tommy. I was the way you are now about Jim. So I made this deal with the playground. Oh, there are others, too. You'll see them among the kids."

"You'd better run home to bed."

"You want it to be true. I saw your eyes then! If you could trade places with Jim, you would. Save him all that torture, let him be in your place, grown-up, the real work over and done."

"Any decent parent sympathizes with his children."

"You more than most. You feel every kick. You come here tomorrow. You can make a deal, too."

"Trade places?" It was an amusing, but an oddly satisfactory thought. "What would I have to do?"

"Just make up your mind." He tried to make it sound casual, a joke. But his mind was in a rage, again, frantic.

"What would I pay?"

"Nothing. You'd just have to play in the playground."

"All day?"

"And go to school, of course."

"And grow up again?"

"Yes. Be here at four."

"I have work in the city tomorrow."

"Tomorrow," said the boy.

"You'd better get home to bed, Tommy."

"My name is *Tom* Marshall," said the boy, sitting there.

The playground lights went out.

Mr. Underhill and his wife did not speak at breakfast. He usually phoned her at noon to chat about this or that, but he did not phone. But at one-thirty, after a bad lunch, he dialed the house number. When Susan answered he hung up. Five minutes later he phoned again.

"Charlie, was that you called five minutes ago?"

"Yes," he said.

"I thought I heard you breathing before you hung up. What'd you call about, dear?" She was being sensible again.

"Oh, just called."

"It's been a bad two days, hasn't it? You do see what I mean, don't you, Charlie? Jim must go to the playground and get a few scabs."

"A few scabs, yes."

He saw the blood and the hungry foxes and the torn rabbits.

"And learn to give and take," she was saying, "and fight if he has to."

"Fight if he has to," he murmured.

"I knew you'd come around."

"Around," he said. "You're right. No way out. He must be sacrificed."

"Oh, Charlie, you're so odd."

He cleared his throat. "Well, that's settled. Love me?"

"Yes."

I wonder what it would be like, he thought.

"Miss me?" he asked the phone.

116

He thought of the diagrams in the dust, the boy seated there with the hidden bones in his face.

"Yes," she said.

"I've been thinking," he said. "The playground."

"Speak up."

"I'll be home at three," he said, slowly, piercing out the words, like a man hit in the stomach, gasping for breath. "We'll take a walk, you and Jim and I," he said, eyes shut.

"Wonderful!"

"To the playground," he said and hung up.

It was really autumn now, the real chill, the real snap, the trees overnight burnt red and snapped free of their leaves, which spiraled about Mr. Underhill's face as he walked up the front steps, and there were Susan and Jim bundled up because of the sharp wind, waiting for him.

"Hello!" they cried to one another, with much embracing and kissing. "There's Jim down there!" "There's Daddy up there!" They laughed and he felt paralyzed and in terror of the late day. It was almost four. He looked at the leaden sky, which might pour down molten silver any moment, a sky of lava and soot and a wet wind blowing out of it. He held his wife's arm very tightly as they walked. "Aren't you friendly, though?" She smiled.

"It's ridiculous, of course," he said, thinking of something else.

"What?"

They were at the playground gate.

"Hello, Charlie. Hi!" Far away, atop the monstrous slide stood the Marshall boy, waving, not smiling now.

"You wait here," said Mr. Underhill to his wife. "I'll only be a moment. I'll just take Jim in."

"All right."

117

He grasped the small boy's hand. "Here we go, Jim. Stick close to Daddy."

They stepped down the hard concrete steps and stood in the flat dust. Before them, in a magical sequence, stood diagrams, gigantic tic-tac-toes, monstrous hopscotches, the amazing numerals and triangles and oblongs of children's scrabbling in the incredible dust.

The sky blew a huge wind upon him and he was shivering. He grasped the little boy's hand still tighter and turned to his wife. "Goodbye!" he said. For he was believing it. He was in the playground and believing it, and it was for the best. Nothing was too good for Jim! Nothing at all in the crazy world! And now his wife was laughing back at him, "Charlie, you idiot!"

They were running, running across the dirt playground floor, at the bottom of a stony sea that pressed and blew upon them. Now Jim was crying, "Daddy, Daddy!" and the children racing to meet them, the boy on the slide yelling, the tic-tac-toe and hopscotches whirling, a sense of bodiless terror gripping him, but he knew what he must do and what must be done and what would happen. Far across the field footballs sailed, baseballs whizzed, bats flew, fists jabbed up, and the door of the Manager's office stood open, the desk empty, the seat empty, a lone light burning in it.

Mr. Underhill stumbled, shut his eyes and fell, crying out, his body clenched by a hot pain, mouthing strange words, everything in turmoil.

"There you are, Jim," said a voice.

And he was climbing, climbing, eyes closed, climbing metal, ringing ladder rungs, screaming, wailing, his throat raw.

Mr. Underhill opened his eyes.

He was on top of the slide. The gigantic slide which was

118

ten thousand feet high, it seemed. Children after him, children beating him to go on, slide! Slide!

And he looked, and there, going off across the field, was a man in a black overcoat. And there, at the gate, was a woman waving and the man standing there with the woman, both of them looking in at him, waving, and their voices calling, "Have a good time! Have a good time, Jim!"

He screamed. He looked at his hands, in a panic of realization. The small hands, the thin hands. He looked at the earth far below. He felt his nose bleeding and there was the Marshall boy next to him. "Hi!" cried the other, and bashed him in the mouth. "Only twelve years here!" cried the other in the uproar.

Twelve years! thought Mr. Underhill, trapped. And time is different to children. A year is like ten years. No, not twelve years of childhood ahead of him, but a century, a century of *this!*

"Slide!"

He was pinched, pummeled and shoved. He felt fists rising, he saw the fox faces, and beyond them, at the fence, the man and woman walking off. He screamed, he shrieked, he covered his face, he felt himself pushed, bleeding, to the rim of nothingness. Face first, he careened down the slide, screeching, with ten thousand monsters behind. A thought jumped through his brain a moment before he hit bottom in a nauseous mound of claws.

This is Hell, this is Hell!

And no one in the hot, milling heap contradicted him.

MARGOT ARNOLD

The Girl in the Mirror

Jennifer Vidler looked around her room with a sigh of boredom.

It was untidy, as usual, but she could not be bothered to tidy it up, even though her mother had been after her to do so. Her friends were always going on about how pretty it was and how lucky she was to have a room like this of her own. Little did *they* know, she thought gloomily. Her eyes wandered over the bleached silver oak fittings: the built-in wardrobe, the desk, the bookshelves and the stand that held her stereo and television set, and moved on to the gracious lines of her white four-poster bed that seemed almost to float on the thick scarlet wall-to-wall carpet.

She went slowly to the window and gazed down at the busy street below. From this height, cars and people looked like large mechanical toys moving jerkily and without purpose. Oh, what she would give to be away from all this, away from the city! Right away in the country. She slipped easily into her favorite daydream—a big farm in the country with her own horse, and a dog, and cats, and rabbits, and lots of space to roam around in, and—oh, everything! Roaming wild and free all day long with the animals . . . A horn honked outside and the dream shattered.

Again she sighed heavily. Here it was, the beginning of the summer holidays, and all she had to look forward to was a measly fortnight in France with her parents. She was almost sorry that school was finally over—not that she liked school that much, but at least it was something to *do.*

She put a David Cassidy record on the turntable and continued her restless ramble around the room. Coming to the dressing table with its glass top and white-flounced frill, she stopped before it and, propping her head in her hands, gazed moodily into the mirror. She had made a fuss about it when her mother had put it in the room, but secretly she rather liked it. It had been one of the "heirlooms" she had inherited from her great-aunt and namesake, Aunt Jennifer, and it did not quite "go" with the rest of the room, being an antique, shield-shaped, swing mirror, standing on its own little stand in which were three small velvet-lined drawers where she kept her most cherished possessions.

Every time she looked into it she would think of Aunt Jennifer, who had been incredibly old but who had always interested her with stories about her long gone youth on a farm in Kent. What especially interested young Jennifer were the stories her great-aunt used to tell about her own grandmother, who had lived on the very same farm way back in the 1830s. She, too, had been a Jennifer, and had had a twin sister called Belinda to whom something terrible had happened.

It had been a very long time before young Jennifer had managed to find out what that terrible thing was, because whenever her great-aunt got to that part, some grown-up—

121

usually her own mother—would break in with, "Now I'm sure you don't want to go into all that, Aunt Jennifer," and their warning glances were enough to tell her that it was something they did not want her to know about. She had imagined all sorts of horrible things so, when at last she had got Aunt Jennifer all to herself and had heard the story, she had been quite disappointed.

"Oh," said Aunt Jennifer vaguely. "About poor Belinda? Yes, well she went quite mad when she was a young girl and had to spend the rest of her life shut up in the farm attic where no one could see her. They didn't know what to do with mad people in those days, you see, and it was a *terrible* disgrace to have one in the family."

"What made her go mad?" Jennifer asked with interest.

Her great-aunt shrugged. "My grandmother never knew for sure. She thought maybe it was because their step-mother was too hard on Belinda, who was a very dreamy kind of girl and who wasn't very helpful about the farm. Anyway, one summer's day Belinda started to act very strangely; she pretended she was Jennifer and talked about all kinds of crazy things like talking boxes and wheels that sang songs, and even about men flying about in the sky. It got so bad that they sent the real Jennifer, my grand-mother, away for a while, and when she came back poor Belinda was chained up in the attic and she was never al-lowed to see her again, even though they were twins—and identical twins at that . . ."

Oh yes, Jennifer sorely missed Aunt Jennifer and her sto-ries, but the old lady had died a few months ago and had left her some very nice things.

The door opened and her mother's face appeared around the crack. "Jennifer, *do* turn down that record player! We'll have the neighbors complaining again." The head swiveled and took in the untidy state of the room. "And for goodness' sake, tidy this mess up, will you? It's the third time I've spoken to you about it." The voice was pained.

"All right," Jennifer said sullenly. Her mother sighed and closed the door with an exasperated click.

"Drat the neighbors!" Jennifer resumed her former position and stared dismally into the mirror. "Oh, how heavenly it must have been to live on that farm, away from everybody!" Her own sad face stared back at her, the long dark hair hanging forward and slightly shadowing its pallor. Then she felt a thrill of amazement, for while the face was the same, the whole room behind was quite different. She glanced quickly over her shoulder to see if her eyes were playing tricks with her, but there was her own room, just the same as it always was. She looked back at the mirror, and the other room was still there—cream walls with great black beams showing in them, and dark, heavy furniture, including a large four-poster bed with a patchwork quilt. And there was a window where no window existed in her room; a window of small, diamond-shaped panes which stood open to show the leaves of a great oak tree dancing in the summer breeze, and there was a door of black oak with a latch instead of a knob on it.

Jennifer took each detail in slowly. How could this be? Here she was looking at her reflection in a strange room! Then she noticed with a shock that while the face was the same, the dress was quite different. The girl in the mirror was wearing a shapeless long dress of some kind of checked cotton, with stupid looking puffed sleeves out of which her thin arms stuck like sticks. Jennifer glanced down at her own stylish nylon blouse and neat Black Watch kilt, then back at the mirror. "Who are you?" she whispered through dry lips. "Why is everything suddenly so different?"

The girl's face—her own face—came a little closer. "Oh, I'm *so* glad you've finally seen me; that you've said something!" The voice was high and thin and clear like a mountain stream. "Now we can talk. Now I can find out about all those wonderful things you have that I can see from here. I've been *dying* to know about them." She gave a delighted laugh that tinkled like a fairy bell. "What *talks* we'll be able to have now!"

"But . . . *where* are you?" Jennifer stammered.

"Why, on Pear Tree Farm, of course, where I've always been." The tinkly laugh broke out again. "And I know who *you* are; there's only one person in the world who looks exactly like me, so you're Jennifer. Don't you know me, silly? I'm Belinda!"

Thrills went up and down Jennifer's spine. "The farm—the old farm! You're actually on it?"

"Of course."

Jennifer looked very carefully at her look-alike, thinking of the sad story she had been told. She certainly did not *look* mad, and besides, behind her was the enchanting prospect of the farm. Belinda would be able to tell her all about it. "Well, I'm not *your* Jennifer," she said cautiously, "but I think I know what has happened. We are both of us caught in a Time Warp—that must be it!" (She was a great fan of *Star Trek,* so knew all about such things.)

"I don't care who you say you are, Jennifer, or what we're caught in, just so long as we can be friends and you can tell me all about those exciting things," Belinda said eagerly.

"I do know one thing, though," Jennifer went on. "We'll have to keep this a *deadly* secret between us. It would never do if anyone else found out."

124

"No, indeed!" Belinda made a face and shivered. "Why, my stepmother is so strict and nasty—well, she'd probably smash this glass if she thought I was having any *fun.*"

So began their strange, looking glass friendship. Jennifer's parents could hardly believe the change in her; instead of complaining all the time as she usually did in the holidays, she seemed perfectly content to stay in her room, and had almost to be pushed out of the flat to get some fresh air. "She really is becoming much more grown-up," her mother said proudly, and as a reward gave her a lovely gold locket with her birthstone set in the middle of it.

As for Jennifer, she could hardly wait to get back to her room and the mirror, and to hear all the marvelous things about the farm. She would get quite cross with Belinda who, after a while, would always say, "I've talked enough. Now *you* tell *me* about your wonderful life." And she could not understand why Belinda should be so impressed by very ordinary things like having a bed all to oneself, and light whenever one needed it, or music at the touch of a switch. "Imagine! Music whenever you want it—what bliss! I do love it so, and there is none here on the farm, none at all," Belinda would say sadly.

But most of all it was her television set that really enchanted Belinda, who could not see enough of it and who made Jennifer very angry when she wanted to watch it instead of talking. She got so fed up with Belinda's constant pleas to see it that she would leave it on when she was not in the room, so that Belinda could watch. She was roundly scolded by her mother for wasting electricity, but she still went on doing it.

On her part, although she never tired of hearing about the two riding horses and the dogs and cats, Jennifer became aware that farm life was not always as nice as she had imagined. Often when she hurried to the mirror Belinda would not be there, and when she did come she would be tired and cross. "I've been working," she would say irritably. "That's all there ever is to do here—work, work, work!" Her hands were always red and raw and quite ugly, but Jennifer was too polite to say so. And she found to her surprise that Belinda was quite ignorant about even the simplest things.

"Don't they teach you *anything* in school," she said crossly, one day when Belinda seemed even denser than usual.

"School?" echoed Belinda. "I don't go to school. That's just for *boys*. Though my grandmother did teach me how to make the alphabet and sign my name on a sampler in needlework—*and* I know my figures," she said proudly. "I can add! You mean *you* go to school just like a boy, all the time?"

"Well, except for holidays," Jennifer agreed. "But it isn't any fun stuck in a stuffy old classroom every day. I *hate* it. You're lucky not to be bothered with it."

But the more they talked, the more they became envious of each other's life and unhappy with their own; especially Belinda, who would lapse into a gloomy silence and gaze longingly into Jennifer's room. One day when she was doing this, Jennifer cast around in her mind for something new to talk about. She opened up one of the velvet-lined drawers under the mirror and held up the new locket. "Look what my mother just gave me," she said.

Belinda brightened up. "Oh, it's just *beautiful*," she gasped, and reached for it. For a second a small misty hand appeared, and suddenly there was the locket on the other side of the mirror, with Belinda laughing and twirling it in the air.

"Hey!" said Jennifer. "You've taken my locket. Give it back!"

Belinda stopped laughing, and a look of wild hope came into her face. "Jenny," she whispered, "it *did* pass through. And if *it* can, maybe *we* can, too! Oh, wouldn't that be fun! I could get into your room and play with all those lovely things, and you could come here and play with the animals—even ride the horses, if you like."

"Well, I don't know," Jennifer said dubiously. "Do you think it would work?"

"Why not? Let's see if I can give the locket back . . ." Again a misty outline appeared, and there was the locket gleaming on the glass top. "See, Jenny! I believe we could. Let's try it. You put your fingers to mine on the glass, and when I say 'Go,' we'll both take two steps forward."

The idea had begun to excite Jennifer. "All right," she said eagerly, then another thought struck her. "But wait a moment! What about our clothes? We'd look pretty weird to anyone else. I mean, what would my mother say if she came in and saw you in that cotton sack thing."

Belinda thought for a minute and chuckled. "Then we'll take our clothes off, and when we get to the other side we'll dress in one another's. Then, when we're ready to come back, we'll change again."

Jennifer's heart pounded with excitement. "Right," she whispered, and started to undress a bit shamefacedly, her fingers trembling nervously. At last they faced one another, giggling self-consciously at the sight. Belinda, two spots of high color in her pale cheeks, stretched out her hands. Jenny did the same and took a step forward. For a second she seemed enveloped in an icy mist, where her sight blurred and her senses numbed, then she was standing in that other room, shivering with cold and fear, but excited beyond belief.

Without waiting to dress herself, she ran to the leaded

127

windows, through which drifted the scent of hay and the sounds of summer. She just *had* to see if everything was as Belinda had said it would be.

Sure enough, there was the paddock and the two horses, the gray and the brown, standing head to tail and lazily swishing away the flies. There was the old black and white sheepdog lying in the shade of the barn, and an orange kitten scampering in and out of the wide barn door. So absorbed was she that she paid no attention to a voice from below that was calling on an ever increasing note of anger: "Belinda! Belin-dah!"

She ran back to the mirror. "Oh, Belinda, it's every bit as wonderful as you said . . ." she began, then stopped dead. The shield shaped glass with its three little drawers stood on a dark oak table, but it did not reflect, as she had expected it to, her own cozy room. Instead, the dark outlines of the farm furniture loomed behind her and—worse—there was no sign of Belinda anywhere.

As she stood there in mounting fear and puzzlement, the dark shape of a stern-faced woman in black appeared in the doorway, crying, "Belinda, you lazy good-for-nothing! How many times have I got to call my lungs out before . . ." She stopped short in her scolding as she saw Jennifer crouching naked before the mirror. *"Now* what are you up to, you fiendish girl?" she cried, storming into the room. "What is the meaning of this wicked nakedness? Wait till I tell your Papa of *this!"*

Jennifer cringed back against the traitorous mirror. "I'm *not* Belinda," she whimpered, her heart pounding with terror. "I'm Jennifer, and I want to go home . . ."

The strange disappearance of Jennifer Vidler remains a mystery. No one—least of all the police, who were eventually called in—could explain how a girl could disappear completely from a sixth floor flat in a large London block; particularly one who apparently was not wearing any of her clothes. At least, this was according to her distracted mother, who had been in the living room of the flat all the time and swore her daughter never left it, clothed or un-clothed.

Nor could they explain why the clothes which she had last been seen wearing were found crumpled in an untidy heap before the dressing table, nor why there appeared to be on them the print of a small, dusty hand, while beside them was a large mound of dust, which had scattered in a fine film over everything when the door had been opened.

Perhaps the most amazing thing of all was that the mirror on the dressing table—which, Jennifer's mother had tear-fully maintained to the skeptical police, had always been kept as bright and as silver as the day it was made—was all blotched and dark, so that no reflection of any kind could be seen in it.

After a while people gave the whole thing up as an insolu-ble mystery, but they all said it was just too bad for poor Jennifer, wherever she had got to. How right they were!

BARBARA WILLIAMSON

The Thing Waiting Outside

A cold wind came down from the hills that night and in their room under the peaked roof the children turned their faces toward the sound.

"It's only the wind," the father said.

"Just the wind," said the mother.

There were two beds in the room, a dresser painted white, and under the windows, a table with small bright chairs.

The walls of the room were light yellow, like the first spring sunlight. In their glow the dolls and fire engines, the pasteboard castle with its miniature knights, even the sad-faced Harlequin puppet shimmered with warmth. The plush animals became as soft as down, and the mane on the rocking horse was a crest of foam.

The children, a boy of eight and a girl of six, were already in their beds. The light glistened on their faces, their pale silken hair. They were beautiful children. Everyone

130

said so, even strangers, and their parents always smiled and placed proud hands on their shining heads.

Now in the yellow light with the wind brushing the windows, the children listened to their father.

He sat on the side of the boy's bed and spoke quietly. The mother sat with the girl, her fingers now and then touching the sleeve of her daughter's nightgown. The faces of both parents were troubled.

The father said, "You do understand about the books? Why I had to take them away?"

The boy did not turn his eyes from his father's face, but he could feel the emptiness of the shelves across the room.

He said, "Will you ever put them back?"

His father laid a hand on the boy's shoulder. "Yes, of course," he said. "In time. I *want* you to read, to enjoy your books." He looked now at the girl and smiled. "I'm very proud of both of you. You read so well and learn so quickly."

The mother smiled too and gave the girl's hand a gentle squeeze.

The father said, "I think maybe this whole thing is my fault. I gave you too many books, encouraged you to read to the point of neglecting other things that are important. So for a while the only books I want you to read are your school books. You'll do other things—paint pictures, play games. I'll teach you chess, I think. You'll both like that."

"And we'll do things together," the mother said. "Take bike rides and walks up into the hills. And when it's spring, we'll have a croquet set on the lawn. And we'll go on picnics."

The children looked at their parents with wide dark eyes. And after a moment the boy said, "That will be nice."

131

"Yes," said the girl. "Nice."

The mother and father glanced at each other and then the father leaned over and cupped a hand under the boy's chin.

"You know now, don't you, that you did not really see and speak to the people in the books. They were only here in your imagination. You did not *see* the Lilliputians or *talk* to the Red Queen. You did not *see* the cave dwellers or *watch* the tiger eat one of them. They were not *here* in this room. You know that now, don't you?"

The boy looked steadily into his father's eyes.

"Yes," he said, "I know."

The girl nodded her head when the father turned to her.

"We know," she said.

"Imagination is a wonderful thing," the father said to both of them. "But it has to be watched, or like a fire it can get out of control. You'll remember that, won't you?"

"Yes," the boy said, and again the girl nodded, her long hair gleaming in the light.

The father smiled and got to his feet. The mother rose too and smoothed the blankets on both beds. Then they each kissed the children good night with little murmurs of love and reassurance.

"Tomorrow," the father said, "we'll make some plans."

"Yes," the children said, and closed their eyes.

After the mother and father were gone and the room was dark, the children lay still for what seemed to them a long time. The wind rattled the windows and beyond the hills the moon began to rise.

At last the girl turned to her brother. "Is it time?" she asked.

The boy didn't answer. Instead, he threw back his blanket and crossed the room to the windows. Below, the fields were silvered by the moon, but the hills were a black hulk against the sky.

"Anything could come down from there," he said. "Anything."

The girl came to stand beside him, and together they looked out into the night and thought about the thing waiting outside.

Then the girl said, "Will you take them the book now?"

"Yes," the boy said.

He turned from the windows and went to the dresser. Kneeling on the floor, he pulled open a bottom drawer and felt carefully beneath the socks and undershirts. The girl came over and knelt beside him. Their white faces flowered in the darkness of the room.

They both smiled when the boy took the book out of its hiding place. They rose from the floor and the boy clasped the book in his arms. He said, "Don't start until I get back."

"Oh, I won't," the girl said. "I wouldn't."

Still holding the book close, the boy went to the door of the room, opened it softly, and stepped out into the hall.

It was a large house and very old, and deep inside it the wind was only a whisper of sound. The boy listened for a moment, then started down the stairs. The carpet was thick under his bare feet and the railing felt as cold as stone beneath his hand.

Downstairs, a faint spicy smell from the day's baking still lingered in the air. He walked to the back of the house, past dark rooms where mirrors winked from the light in the hall, and night lay thick across the floors.

The mother and father were in the room next to the kitchen. There was a fire in a small grate and empty coffee cups on a table. On the walls were photographs of the children. They looked out into the room with secret smiles.

133

The mother was seated on the sofa near a shaded lamp. Her lap was full of pink yarn and her knitting needles flashed in the firelight.

The father leaned back in a big leather chair, his eyes on the ceiling, his fingers curled around the bowl of his favorite pipe.

The fire sighed and sparks rose up the chimney. The boy's eyes flicked to the corners of the room where the shadows had retreated from the firelight.

From the doorway he said, "I couldn't sleep until I brought you this." And he went into the room toward his parents, holding the book out to them.

"I hid it, but that wasn't right, was it?"

They came to him then. His mother took him into her arms and kissed him, and his father said that he was a fine honest boy.

The mother held him in her lap for a few minutes and warmed his feet with her hands, and her eyes glistened in the light of the fire. They spoke softly to him for a time and he listened and answered "yes" and "no" at the right times, and then he yawned and said that he was sleepy and could he please go back to bed?

They took him to the stairs and kissed him and he went up alone without looking back.

In the room at the top of the house the girl was waiting for him. He nodded his head and then they climbed into their beds and joined hands across the narrow space between. Moonlight lay on the floor in cold slabs and the wind now washed against the windows with a shushing sound.

"Now," the boy said, gripping the girl's hand tightly. "And, remember, it's harder when the book is somewhere else."

They did not move for a long time. Their eyes stared at

the ceiling without blinking. Sweat began to glisten on their faces and their breathing grew short and labored. The room flowed around them. Shadow and light merged and parted like streams in the sea.

When the sounds from below began to reach them, they still did not move. Their joined hands, slick with sweat, held firm. Their muscles strained and corded. Their eyes burned and swam with the shifting light and darkness.

At last the sounds from the bottom of the house stopped. Silence fell around them, cooling their faces, soothing their feverish eyes.

The boy listened and then said, "It's done. You know what to do now, don't you?"

"Yes," the girl said. She slid her hand out of his, brushed her hair back from her face, and closed her eyes. She smiled and thought of a garden filled with flowers. There was a table in the center of the garden and on the table were china plates. Each plate held a rainbow of iced cakes. There were pink ones and yellow ones and some thick with chocolate. Her tongue flicked over her lips as she thought of how sweet they would taste.

The boy thought of ships—tall ships with white sails. He brought a warm wind out of the south and sent the ships tossing on a sea that was both blue and green. Waves foamed over the decks and the sailors slipped and laughed, while above their heads gulls wheeled in the sky, their wings flashing in the sun.

At the time agreed upon, just as the windows began to lighten, the children rose from their beds and went downstairs.

The house was very cold. The shadows were turning to gray and in the room next to the kitchen the fire was dead, its coals turned to feathery ash.

135

The mother lay in a corner of the room, near the outside wall. The father was a few feet away. He still held the fireplace poker in his hand.

The boy's eyes moved over the room quickly. "I'll find the book," he said. "You go open the door to the terrace."

"Why that one?"

The boy gave her a hard look. "Because that's the one with the catch that slips. It had to get in some way, didn't it?"

The girl turned, then she looked back and said, "Then can we have breakfast?"

The boy had begun moving around the room, looking under tables, poking under the sofa. "There's no time," he said.

"But I'm hungry!"

"I don't care," the boy said. "It's the cleaning lady's day and we have to be asleep when she gets here. We'll eat later."

"Maybe pancakes? With syrup?"

The boy didn't look at her. "Maybe," he said. "Now go open the door like I told you."

The girl stuck her tongue out at him. "I wish I was the oldest," she said.

"Well, you're not," the boy said, turning and glaring at her. "Now go and do like I said."

The girl tossed her hair back in a gesture of defiance, but she left the room, not hurrying, and in the hall she began to hum a little tune to annoy him.

The boy did not notice. He was becoming anxious now. Where could the book be? It wasn't on the table. And it couldn't be out of the room. He saw it then, on the floor, under the shattered lamp.

He hurried to it and his hands were shaking when he

picked it up, brushing the bits of glass away. He examined it carefully, turning the pages, running his fingers over the smooth binding, the embossed letters of that title. Then he smiled. It was all right. There weren't even any spatters of blood.

He closed the covers and hugged the book to his chest. A great joy welled inside him. It was one of his favorite stories. Very soon, he promised himself, he would read *The Hound of the Baskervilles* again.

JANE SPEED

Fair's Fair

I knew right away Mother had something besides breakfast on her mind when she set a bowl of oatmeal in front of me. I mean it was *Saturday*. She usually gives that "busy little engines need good fuel" stuff a rest on Saturdays and lets me have whatever I want.

I was still wondering if it would do me any good to point this out to her when Daddy came in and sat down at the table. So I decided to just put a lot of strawberry jam on the oatmeal to pep it up and not say anything. Maybe, if I kept quiet, Mother would halfway forget I was there and go ahead and talk to Daddy about whatever was bothering her. Of course, it might be just bills. You'd be surprised how worked up my parents can get on *that* subject sometimes.

Daddy drank his juice down in one gulp like he always does and picked up the morning paper. But I could tell by the way Mother was stirring and stirring her coffee that he wasn't going to get much read.

Sure enough, in about half a minute she said, "Harry—"

He just said, "Hm?" and kept his head behind the paper, although he must have known already that it was a lost cause.

"Herbert Wellman's mother died last week."

"Did she now?" Daddy folded the paper and put it aside then.

It actually took me a couple of seconds to figure out who Herbert Wellman was. That may sound funny because the Wellmans live right next door to us. But I sometimes forget their name because Jeddie Brubaker always calls Mrs. Wellman the Cat Lady. That's because she likes cats so much. She has a couple of her own and every night she puts bowls of milk and scraps out for all the strays in the neighborhood. I know because my bedroom is over our kitchen and I watch her sometimes from my window taking the stuff down their steep old back porch steps.

Some nights they get to howling and fighting out back—the cats, I mean—and Daddy wanted to complain about it once but Mother wouldn't let him. She said cats were all poor Isobel Wellman had. She had no children and she hardly even had a husband. And it does seem that way because Mr. Wellman is almost never there.

He comes home late every night, sometimes not till after I'm in bed, and he's never there on weekends at all. On weekends he always goes to look after his mother's place. It's in a little town called Penn Oaks about fifty miles from here. Only I suppose now she's dead he won't be doing that anymore.

"Well, it's about time—" Daddy began, then the way he stopped all of a sudden I knew without looking that Mother must have given him the old "little pitchers have big ears" signal.

"Amy, dear," she said to me in that phony bright kind of

voice she always uses when she's going to try to talk me into something I don't particularly want to do. "It's such a lovely morning, why don't you go on outside and play?"

Wouldn't you know? Just when things were getting interesting. Still—she didn't seem to notice that I hadn't finished my oatmeal (frankly, that strawberry jam didn't work out too well), so I just slid off my chair and went out the screen door.

I made as much noise as possible going down the back steps, then I tiptoed around and hoisted myself up onto the garbage can under the open breakfast room window. I'd hardly missed a thing.

"—what it's going to be like for Isobel now," Mother was saying, "having him home on weekends."

"Well—fine, I should think. I mean, isn't that what you've been complaining about all these years?—his spending every spare minute at his mother's and leaving poor Isobel with nothing but those damn cats. Oh, I agree, I agree," Daddy said this last part kind of fast as though Mother had started to interrupt him. "That's no way to treat a wife. But Herb had his problems, too, with that mother of his. She must have been a real Tartar—wouldn't budge out of the old house and yet she refused to hire anyone to look after things for her. So—now she's gone. Maybe Herb and Isobel can finally settle down and lead a normal life."

"I just hope," Mother said, kind of gloomy and mysterious, "it isn't too late."

"Now what the devil do you mean by that?"

"Oh, Harry! They've been living that way for fifteen *years*. People can't just snap back and forth like—like puppets."

For a minute neither of them said anything, then Mother started again and her voice sounded different, sort of quiet.

"Have you forgotten what Isobel Wellman was like when they first moved here? How pretty she was?"

I nearly fell off the garbage can when she said that. You should *see* Mrs. Wellman. For one thing, her fingernails are always a lot dirtier than my mother'd ever let me get away with. That's because next to cats she likes gardening best of all, and she doesn't wear garden gloves because she says she likes the feel of the soil.

This year she's got a lot of sweet peas that she's really crazy about. They *are* sort of pretty—kind of a pinkish lavender. But not Mrs. Wellman. I mean she's okay to talk to and all that, but she's not *pretty*. She's all caved-in looking and beaky nosed and her hair goes every which way as though she never combed it.

Jeddie Brubaker says she's a witch. And you know something? I used to halfway believe it was true. That's when I was a lot younger, of course. But Mrs. Wellman used to do all kinds of cooking and baking and I guess she had more than she needed because she was always handing stuff out to the neighborhood kids. For a long time I was afraid to take anything from her for fear it would cast a spell on me or something.

Then one time Jeddie dared me to take a cookie and eat it right there. And I did and it was pretty good. Not as good as my mother's, but at least I didn't fall down in a fit or anything. You just can't believe half of what that klunky kid says.

"And how hard she tried," Mother was really going strong now, "to make a nice home for that man. The meals she used to cook—and then he never came home for them. After a while she just gave up and made the best life she could out of those cats and her garden. What I'm trying to

141

say is, I think she's come to *count* on Herb's not being there."

"Oh, Madge." I heard Daddy's chair scrape back. "I really think you're making too much out of this. They'll work things out. People do, you know."

Mother gave a big sigh and said, "I hope you're right." Then she got up, too, and started clearing off the table, so I slid down off the garbage can in a hurry and ran back and got myself going in the old rope swing in case Daddy looked out back to see what I was doing.

After a while he and Mother both came out and he said he was going to drive her over to the shopping center to get some groceries and did I want to come along. But I'd already spent my allowance and it's kind of boring just hanging around over there if you can't buy anything, so I decided to stay home. I pumped myself up good and high so I could wave to them all the way out the driveway, then I just let the swing glide almost to a stop.

All of a sudden out of nowhere Marmy jumped into my lap. She's one of Mrs. Wellman's cats, my favorite. I used to think Mrs. Wellman got the name out of *Little Women*. It would fit, too, because Marmy's always being a mother. Almost every time you turn around she's got another litter of kittens.

But Mrs. Wellman said she named her that because she's what's called a marmalade cat, kind of splotchy yellow all over. She's not much to look at—Marmy, I mean. She's small, for one thing, and she stays skinny even though Mrs. Wellman feeds her a lot, and she kind of sags in the middle.

But I like her because she's so smart. She really knows who's her friend and who isn't. Right now, if my father was home and came out the back door she'd be off like a streak. Daddy wouldn't *do* anything mean to her, you understand, but she just knows somehow that he doesn't really care for cats.

Not like that dumb Beau. That's Mrs. Wellman's other cat, Beau Brummel. He's Marmy's son but he's about three times as big as she is. He's tiger except for a patch of white on his chest, really a big handsome tom. But he's all looks and no brains. Or else he's just so conceited he's sure everyone is going to admire him.

Honestly, that cat never learns. Like with Jeddie Brubaker. Jeddie's always tormenting Beau; he actually tied a can to his tail once, but Beau still comes right up and rubs against his legs. You wouldn't catch Marmy within a mile of that pest—Jeddie, I mean.

Marmy was licking my hand with her scratchy tongue and purring away like an engine. Then suddenly she stopped and arched her back, and in one leap she took off up the trunk of the tree and disappeared in the branches. I couldn't figure out at first what had scared her, then I looked over next door and I saw that Mr. Wellman had come out on their back porch.

I'd never got a really good look at him in the daytime before. I saw him from my window last night, though, and I know why Marmy ran. Mr. Wellman doesn't like cats. Last night he came out on the porch in his pajamas and bathrobe, smoking a cigar. Then he looked down and saw the stuff Mrs. Wellman had put out for the strays.

He stomped down the steps like he was real mad and dumped out the milk and put the scraps in the garbage can. And as he went back inside I heard him yelling to Mrs. Wellman that she wasn't to do that anymore; he'd had enough of those yowling cats cluttering up the backyard.

He just stood there now, looking around and frowning as

though he didn't much like anything he saw. I guess he was still unhappy because his mother died.

Then I saw Beau. He was walking along the porch railing toward Mr. Wellman, slow and fancy like a tightrope walker. And I knew just what he had in mind. I wanted to call out and warn Beau, but it wouldn't have done any good with that stupid cat.

Sure enough, Beau jumped down right in front of Mr. Wellman and started rubbing against his legs. Mr. Wellman jerked away and said a really bad word. Then, before I knew what was happening, he pulled his leg back and brought it forward hard. The toe of his shoe caught Beau right smack in the stomach.

Beau let out an awful howl and went sailing out over the steps like he was flying. He landed on his feet all right, but not for long. He kind of staggered around and then fell over on his side, and all the time he kept up such a terrible howling I wanted to put my hands over my ears. Only I didn't dare move even an inch for fear Mr. Wellman would look over and see me there. If he could do a thing like that to Beau—

All at once Beau stopped howling. A sort of a big shiver ran all through him, and then he just lay still. Mr. Wellman started down a couple of steps and just then Mrs. Wellman came out the back door. Before she could say anything he turned around to her and said, "Isobel, I'm sorry. But that damned cat cut right across my feet as I was walking down the steps. I couldn't help tripping over him. It's a miracle we're not both down there."

That—just—wasn't—*so*. Mr. Wellman had been standing on the porch. I saw him. He wasn't going down the steps at all. I don't know whether Mrs. Wellman believed him or not. She didn't say anything. She just went down the steps

144

past him and knelt beside Beau and stroked him for a minute. I think she was crying, but she didn't make any noise.

Then she got up and went back under the steps and brought out a spade, and very gently she lifted up that big old cat in her arms.

For some reason that made Mr. Wellman mad. He stomped down the steps and said, "Oh, for God's sake, stop making such a tragedy of it." And he grabbed Beau and the spade right out of her hands and started to the back of the yard.

I was scared he was going to stop near where I was, but he kept right on going. And then I saw where he was headed. He could have buried Beau anywhere in that whole *yard,* but instead he got down right in front of Mrs. Wellman's sweet pea bed and started chopping at it, digging fast. When he had a hole big enough, he just threw Beau in like a sack of garbage, then he covered him over with dirt and that tangle of pulled-up sweet peas.

All the time Mrs. Wellman just stood there watching him. She never said a word. Once, though, she rubbed her hands down the sides of her skirt as though her legs hurt her.

Mr. Wellman got up and went back without even looking at her. He threw the spade in the tool basket, then he went up the steps and in the door, letting it slam behind him. And after a couple of minutes Mrs. Wellman went inside, too.

As soon as they'd gone I got off the swing and ran into our house as fast as I could. It surely did seem empty. I wondered what was taking my parents so long. I began to think maybe they'd had an accident and been killed and I'd have to live in this house all alone next door to Mr. Wellman for the rest of my life.

I was never so glad to hear anything as our car driving in.

As soon as my parents came into the kitchen Daddy asked me, the way he always does, "Anything exciting happen while we were gone?" It's a kind of a game and I always make up a lot of stuff, just silly, you know—he isn't supposed to believe it.

Only today, when something really did happen, I couldn't think of a thing to say. Daddy looked at me kind of funny for a minute, then he shrugged and went on helping Mother put away the groceries. I guess he thought I was just tired of the game.

I hung around inside the rest of the day. To tell the truth, I was afraid if I went out I might run into Mr. Wellman and I was sure if he took one look at me he'd know I knew what he did to Beau and how he'd lied about it.

Mother noticed after a while and she began to worry that I was coming down with something. She felt my forehead and took my temperature, and pretty soon after supper she said I'd better go up to bed and get a good night's sleep. When I didn't put up a fight, Daddy said I really *must* be sick.

Mother kissed me goodnight and said I could read a little while if I wanted to, so I finished my library book. But even after I'd turned off the light I didn't feel really sleepy.

I got out of bed and went over to the window to see if anything was happening next door. There was a light on in the Wellmans' kitchen, but everything seemed quiet. Then I looked down at the bottom of the steps and there, just like always, was a big bowl of milk and a plate of scraps. Mrs. Wellman must have forgotten about what Mr. Wellman told her last night. Boy, if he saw that he was really going to be mad!

I was just hoping and hoping he'd go right up to bed and not come out on the porch. But just then a puff of smoke came through the screen door and Mr. Wellman pushed it open and came out. He stood there smoking for a while just like last night. Then he must have looked down and seen the food because he let out a roar and started for the steps. But before he even got down to the first one he sort of pitched forward.

He didn't go flying like Beau because he was so big and heavy. He just fell straight down and his head knocked over the bowl of milk. I waited to see if he was going to get up and stagger around, but he didn't. So I decided I'd better go tell somebody what happened because he must be pretty badly hurt. His neck looked all bent around, the wrong way sort of.

But I didn't have to after all because just then Mrs. Wellman came out the back door. She must have heard him call out. She stood there and looked at him for a minute and then she did the funniest thing. She stooped down by the railing at one side of the steps and untied something—string, I guess—and very carefully, like she wanted to save it, she wrapped it around her fingers all the way across the steps and untied it at the other side. Then she stood up and tucked it into her pocket.

I thought maybe then she'd go down to see about Mr. Wellman, but she didn't. She just went back inside the house.

Almost right away our telephone started ringing. And after about a minute I heard my father running down our back steps. He went across the driveway and knelt down beside Mr. Wellman. And when Mrs. Wellman came out again he talked to her for a couple of minutes, then he went with her inside their house.

Pretty soon a police car came up and then an ambulance, and everybody poked around at Mr. Wellman and they

147

talked some more. And then finally they put Mr. Wellman on a stretcher and covered him all up and took him away.

For a long time after I got back into bed I lay there wondering if I ought to tell Daddy what I saw. I know Mr. Wellman didn't fall down the steps by accident. But then—what happened to Beau wasn't an accident either. So if I didn't tell on Mr. Wellman, why should I tell on Mrs. Wellman? After all, fair's fair.

H. R. F. KEATING

A Hell of
a Story

T hey snatched the Oil Sheik's kid, exactly as planned, at 11:06 precisely. There were no difficulties. The girl they'd got for the job distracted the boy's body-guard for just long enough. The boy himself reacted to the little flying helicopter on a string just as they'd calculated he would. But then a kid of eight, and an Arab from the sticks first time in London, that part couldn't have gone wrong. Worth every penny of all it had cost, that toy.

Everything else had gone like clockwork, too. No traffic holdups when they were moving away from the park. No trouble in the changeover of cars. No one about in the mews to see it, and not a bit of fuss out of the lad. Quiet, big eyed, doing what he was told, scared to death most likely.

So inside half an hour he was safely in the room they'd prepared for him in the old house waiting for demolition up over Kilburn way. No one had spotted them taking him in. He hadn't had time to see enough of the outside of the place to remember it again when they'd got the cash and let

149

him go. And Old Pete was there minding him. Dead right for the job.

Forty years in and out of the nick had soured Old Pete to such a point that anybody who met him accidentally began at once to think how they could get away. No one would come poking their nose into the Kilburn place when there was sixteen stone of Old Pete there, fat but hard, never much of a one for shaving, always a bit of a smell to him. The kid was in as safe hands as could be while they conducted the negotiations.

They put in the first call to the rented Mayfair house at six o'clock that evening when they calculated the Sheik would have had just about enough time to have unpleasant thoughts and be ready quietly to agree to dodge the police and pay up. "The kid's safe," they said. "He'll be having his supper now. He's being well looked after."

It was true. Old Pete was just going into the room with the boy's supper, baked beans and a cup of tea, prepared on the picnic stove they'd put into the place. The boy looked at the extraordinary food—extraordinary to him—without seeming to be much put out by it. Old Pete even grunted a question at him, which he hadn't meant to. Only the kid's calm was a bit unexpected. It threw Old Pete a little. "All right, are you?" he grunted.

The boy looked at him, his large dark eyes clear and unwavering.

"Will you mind being in Hell?" he asked.

Old Pete, lumbering toward the door with its dangling padlock, stopped dead in his tracks and turned round.

"English," he said dazedly. "English. You speak English."

"Of course I do," the boy replied. "I always speak English with the Adviser. Talking with me is all he has to do, now that my father has the oil and doesn't need advice any-more."

Old Pete, crafty enough in his way but not one for con-fronting new situations easily, stood blinking, trying to fit this into the framework of his knowledge. And there was something else. Something at the back of his mind that had to be dealt with, too. And it was that, surprisingly, that pushed itself forward first.

"'Ere," he said suddenly, "what d'you mean 'Hell'?"

"Will you mind being in Hell forever?" the boy asked.

"What d'you mean, me being in Hell?"

"Well, you will have to go there. Kidnapping is a sin. If you commit sins you go to Hell."

The simple, fundamental philosophy of the desert fell like drops of untarnished water from his lips.

Old Pete, tire tummied, dirt engrimed, looked at the kid for a long while without speaking a word. Then at last the machinery of his mind ground out his answer.

"Look, lad," he said, "that's all gone out. They finished with all that. Word may've not got round to where you come from, but they found out all that's wrong. Just tales. You know, what ain't so."

He stood, bending forward a little, examining the slight form of the boy in his neat, expensive Western shirt and shorts.

"Yes," he said, ramming it home, "you take my word for it, lad. That's all pastimes stuff now. Gone and forgotten."

He made his way out, an evil-smelling forty-ton tank, and carefully refitted the padlock to the little secure room.

But the next morning, when the Sheik was still holding out and the rest of them were considering what would be the easiest way of putting the pressure on a bit, the boy proved not to have absorbed the latest developments in Western thought at all. When Old Pete brought him his breakfast, the kid accepted the big bowl of cornflakes eagerly enough, but in his conversation he was making no concessions to modernity.

"You will go to Hell, you know," he said, picking up from where they had left off. "You have to—you've done wrong."

"But I told yer," said Old Pete. "They changed all that."

"You can't," the boy said, with all the calm certainty of someone pointing out an accidental breach in the rules of a game. "If you do something wrong, you have to be punished for it. Isn't that so?"

"Well, I don't know about that," said Pete. "I mean, the cops don't always catch you. Not if you're sharp. They're not going to catch us for this lot, that's for sure. Those boys has it worked out a right treat."

"Yes," said the Sheik's son, "but that's just the reason."

"Just the reason?"

"Yes, if you do not get caught and punished here, you must be punished when you are dead. When you cross the Bridge of Al Sirat, which is only as wide as the breadth of a hair, the weight of your sin makes you fall. Into Hell."

His large brown eyes looked steadily into Pete's battered face.

"It's forever, of course," the boy added.

Old Pete left the room in too much of a hurry to collect last night's dirty baked beans plate.

He did not come back at lunchtime as he had meant to do. But at about six that evening—when the Sheik, after talk of making life hard for the boy, had just caved in and promised to deliver the cash—Old Pete once more removed the heavy padlock on the door and entered with another plate of steaming baked beans. The boy said nothing but seized eagerly on the beans. Old Pete turned to the door. But then he stopped, and began to gather up the two previous lots of dirty crockery. The boy ate steadily. Pete picked up the plates and put them down again. At last he broke out.

"Forever?" he said.

"Of course," the boy answered, knowing at once what they were talking about. "If you go to Paradise forever if you've been good, then you must go to Hell forever if you've been bad."

"Yeah," said Pete. And after a little he added, "Stands to reason, I suppose."

He put the now emptied second baked beans plate on top of the others.

"I'm not meant to tell yer," he said, "but you'll be going back 'ome soon. Yer old man's coming up with the dibbins."

"It won't make any difference," the boy said, again answering an unspoken question.

Pete blundered out of the room, snapping the big padlock closed with a ferocious click. And entirely forgetting the dirty crockery.

But he was back within twenty minutes.

"Look," he said. "If I'd forgotten to lock the door when I brought you your nosh just now, you could've sneaked out and nobody the wiser."

"No," said the boy. "You must *take* me home, all the way. Otherwise it wouldn't count."

Sweat broke out under the dirt of Pete's broad, fat bulged face. "I can't do that. They'd catch me. Catch me for sure."

At the steps leading up to the door of the big corner house in Mayfair the boy turned to his companion.

"All right," he said. "I will ring myself. You can go now."

Pete swung away and lumbered off round the corner, fast as if he was a tanker lorry out of control on an ice-slippery hill. But his legs were too jelly-like to support him for long, and once safely round the corner out of sight, he just had to stop and lean against the tall iron railing and let the waves of trembling flow over him.

For two whole minutes he did nothing but lean there, shaking. Then he began to relieve his feelings in dredging up from a well stored memory every foul word he had ever heard. He only came to a halt, after some ten minutes, in order to draw breath.

When he did so the cool, clear, horribly familiar voice of the boy spoke from the open window over his head.

"I'm afraid with all that you will have to go to Hell after all," the boy said.

ROALD DAHL

The Wish

U nder the palm of one hand the child became aware
of the scab of an old cut on his kneecap. He bent
forward to examine it closely. A scab was always a
fascinating thing; it presented a special challenge he was
never able to resist.

Yes, he thought, I will pick it off, even if it isn't ready,
even if the middle of it sticks, even if it hurts like anything.

With a fingernail he began to explore cautiously around
the edges of the scab. He got the nail underneath it, and
when he raised it, but ever so slightly, it suddenly came off,
the whole hard brown scab came off beautifully, leaving an
interesting little circle of smooth red skin.

Nice. Very nice indeed. He rubbed the circle and it didn't
hurt. He picked up the scab, put it on his thigh and flipped it
with a finger so that it flew away and landed on the edge of
the carpet, the enormous red and black and yellow carpet
that stretched the whole length of the hall from the stairs on
which he sat to the front door in the distance. A tremendous

carpet. Bigger than the tennis lawn. Much bigger than that. He regarded it gravely, settling his eyes upon it with mild pleasure. He had never really noticed it before, but now, all of a sudden, the colors seemed to brighten mysteriously and spring out at him in a most dazzling way.

You see, he told himself, I know how it is. The red parts of the carpet are red-hot lumps of coal. What I must do is this: I must walk all the way along it to the front door without touching them. If I touch the red I will be burnt. As a matter of fact, I will be burnt up completely. And the black parts of the carpet . . . yes, the black parts are snakes, poisonous snakes, adders mostly, and cobras, thick like tree trunks round the middle, and if I touch one of *them*, I'll be bitten and I'll die before tea time. And if I get across safely, without being burnt and without being bitten, I will be given a puppy for my birthday tomorrow.

He got to his feet and climbed higher up the stairs to obtain a better view of this vast tapestry of color and death. Was it possible? Was there enough yellow? Yellow was the only color he was allowed to walk on. Could it be done? This was not a journey to be undertaken lightly; the risks were too great for that. The child's face—a fringe of white-gold hair, two large blue eyes, a small pointed chin—peered down anxiously over the banisters. The yellow was a bit thin in places and there were one or two widish gaps, but it did seem to go all the way along to the other end. For someone who had only yesterday triumphantly traveled the whole length of the brick path from the stables to the summer house without touching the cracks, this carpet thing should not be too difficult. Except for the snakes. The mere thought of snakes sent a fine electricity of fear running like pins down the backs of his legs and under the soles of his feet.

He came slowly down the stairs and advanced to the edge of the carpet. He extended one small sandaled foot and placed it cautiously upon a patch of yellow. Then he brought the other foot up, and there was just enough room for him to stand with the two feet together. There! He had started! His bright oval face was curiously intent, a shade whiter perhaps than before, and he was holding his arms out sideways to assist his balance. He took another step, lifting his foot high over a patch of black, aiming carefully with his toe for a narrow channel of yellow on the other side. When he had completed the second step he paused to rest, standing very stiff and still. The narrow channel of yellow ran forward unbroken for at least five yards and he advanced gingerly along it, bit by bit, as though walking a tightrope. Where it finally curled off sideways, he had to take another long stride, this time over a vicious looking mixture of black and red. Halfway across he began to wobble. He waved his arms around wildly, windmill fashion, to keep his balance, and he got across safely and rested again on the other side. He was quite breathless now, and so tense he stood high on his toes all the time, arms out sideways, fists clenched. He was on a big safe island of yellow. There was lots of room on it, he couldn't possibly fall off, and he stood there resting, hesitating, waiting, wishing he could stay forever on this big safe yellow island. But the fear of not getting the puppy compelled him to go on.

Step by step, he edged further ahead, and between each one he paused to decide exactly where next he should put his foot. Once, he had a choice of ways, either to left or right, and he chose the left because although it seemed the more difficult, there was not so much black in that direction. The black was what made him nervous. He glanced quickly over his shoulder to see how far he had come.

Nearly halfway. There could be no turning back now. He was in the middle and he couldn't turn back and he couldn't jump off sideways either because it was too far, and when he looked at all the red and all the black that lay ahead of him, he felt that old sudden sickening surge of panic in his chest—like last Easter time, that afternoon when he got lost all alone in the darkest part of Piper's Wood.

He took another step, placing his foot carefully upon the only little piece of yellow within reach, and this time the point of the foot came within a centimeter of some black. It wasn't touching the black, he could see it wasn't touching, he could see the small line of yellow separating the toe of his sandal from the black; but the snake stirred as though sensing the nearness, and raised its head and gazed at the foot with bright beady eyes, watching to see if it was going to touch.

"I'm not touching you! You mustn't bite me! You know I'm not touching you!"

Another snake slid up noiselessly beside the first, raised its head, two heads now, two pairs of eyes staring at the foot, gazing at a little naked place just below the sandal strap where the skin showed through. The child went high up on his toes and stayed there, frozen stiff with terror. It was minutes before he dared to move again.

The next step would have to be a really long one. There was this deep curling river of black that ran clear across the width of the carpet, and he was forced by his position to cross it at its widest part. He thought first of trying to jump it, but decided he couldn't be sure of landing accurately on the narrow band of yellow the other side. He took a deep breath, lifted one foot, and inch by inch he pushed it out in front of him, far far out, then down and down until at last the tip of his sandal was across and resting safely on the edge of the yellow. He leaned forward, transferring his weight to this front foot. Then he tried to bring the back foot up as well. He strained and pulled and jerked his body, but the legs were too wide apart and he couldn't make it. He tried to get back again. He couldn't do that either. He was doing the splits and he was properly stuck. He glanced down and saw this deep curling river of black underneath him. Parts of it were stirring now, and uncoiling and sliding and beginning to shine with a dreadful oily glister. He wobbled, waved his arms frantically to keep his balance, but that seemed to make it worse. He was starting to go over. He was going over to the right, quite slowly he was going over, then faster and faster, and at the last moment, instinctively he put out a hand to break the fall and the next thing he saw was this bare hand of his going right into the middle of a great glistening mass of black and he gave one piercing cry of terror as it touched.

Outside in the sunshine, far away behind the house, the mother was looking for her son.